Penguin Books

THE HOUSE ON THE BRINK

Two people, a man and a woman, were walking in the fenland, flat as the sea. The grass was coarse where they walked, but beyond it the mud gently humped like the backs of seals – except in one place where something jutted out.

'What's that?' she said.

He looked where she pointed. 'Don't know,' he said. 'Stump or something.'

'Tom!' It was almost a cry. 'It's a body.'

He laughed and held her hand. 'It's not big enough. Your imagination!' he said, 'It even gets me going at times.'

But Tom wasn't the only one to be infected by Mrs Knowles's terrors, Dick Dodds and his new girl friend Helen felt the same chill whenever they came across the sinister log of wood that seemed to have heaved itself up out of the mud and go stumbling and lurching across country by night.

Just *what* was it all about? Was Mr Miller the lawyer trying to frighten Mrs Knowles to death with her own fears? Or was the black stump really moved by some implacable and ghostly purpose in which they were dangerously interfering?

John Gordon, author of *The Giant Under the Snow* which is available as a Puffin, poses many problems in this rather adult and enigmatic book which are only unravelled at the very end, and are echoed by the complicated ebb and flow in Dick's and Helen's new-found friendship.

John Gordon was born in Jarrow, the son of a schoolmaster. His family moved to Wisbech in Cambridgeshire just before the war and he attended the grammar school there until joining the navy during the war. When he was demobbed in 1947, he got a job as a reporter in Wisbech. He has worked on newspapers in Bury St Edmunds, Plymouth and Norwich, where in 1985 he gave up his job as a sub-editor with the *Eastern Evening News* to concentrate on writing. He is married and has two children.

John Gordon

The House on the Brink

Penguin Books
by arrangement with Hutchinson of London

PENGUIN BOOKS

Published by the Penguin Group
27 Wrights Lane, London w8 5tz, England
Viking Penguin Inc., 40 West 23rd Street, New York, New York 10010, USA
Penguin Books Australia Ltd, Ringwood, Victoria, Australia
Penguin Books Canada Ltd, 2801 John Street, Markham, Ontario, Canada l3r 1b4
Penguin Books (NZ) Ltd, 182–190 Wairau Road, Auckland 10, New Zealand

Penguin Books Ltd, Registered Offices: Harmondsworth, Middlesex, England

First published by Hutchinson 1970
Published in Peacock Books 1972
Reprinted in Puffin Books 1982
Reprinted in Penguin Books 1989
10 9 8 7 6 5 4 3 2 1

Copyright © John Gordon, 1970
All rights reserved

Made and printed in Great Britain by
Hazell Watson & Viney Limited
Member of BPCC plc
Aylesbury, Bucks, England
Set in Linotype Pilgrim

For Sylvia

I

The fenland was as flat as the sea. The woman walking on the low bank turned to look behind her. A line of distant trees was like the shadow under the lip of a wave about to roll in from the horizon. There was nothing to stop it. The heat of the day was intense but she shuddered.

There was a man with her, a little way ahead. He raised his arms and drank in the air. 'Marvellous!' he said.

She turned to look in the other direction. The flat land reached away into the sea itself, turning first into sleek mud before, far away, the glazed sea lay over it.

'Marvellous!' said the man again.

The grass was coarse where they walked, but beyond the bank it lay in lush green clots smoothed and limp where the tide had left them. And then the mud gently humped like the backs of seals. Except in one place. Something jutted, rounded but ungainly.

'What's that?' she said.

He looked where she pointed. 'Don't know,' he said. 'Stump or something.'

'Tom!' It was almost a cry. It made his head jerk round towards her. 'It's a body!'

He laughed and held her hand. 'It's not big enough.'

'But it is! Can't you see?'

'No, no, no.' He comforted her, but she would not be

convinced. 'All right, I'll prove it,' he said, and he began to take off his shoes.

'You can't go out there, Tom. It's dangerous. Please don't.'

But he was barefoot, slithering down the bank. The brown mud squeezed up between his toes and engulfed his white feet. 'It's deep,' he said, and bent to roll up his trouser legs.

The woman on the bank bit the knuckles of one clenched fist but said nothing.

He stood up and began to walk. The mud was cold and hugged his feet, reluctant to let him move. It got deeper and he wanted to turn back, but pride made him go on.

The stump was almost black. It lay at an angle, only partly above the mud, and dark weed clung to it like sparse hair. Like hair. But it was still too small for a body.

The mud was up to his knees and he was moving unsteadily. The last few yards were going to be difficult.

'Don't touch it!' Her voice from behind him was as thin as the wind through grass.

Without turning round he waved to reassure her.

Suddenly his raised hand was clenched as though he was fighting to keep his balance. She could not see his face. The corners of his mouth were pulled back in a snarl, his eyes stared, white-rimmed. For the stump was moving, turning like a black finger to point at him. Slowly, slowly, and his feet were trapped.

'Aaaaaaah!' The sound in his throat was too small to reach her but she could see the stump. The blunt end of it seemed for another second to seek him and then suddenly it went blind. A slight quiver and it laid itself gently down. He looked at it, panting. A waterlogged stump.

Since the last tide it had been on the point of overbalancing. He had disturbed the mud and laid it to rest.

'Come back!' She was pleading.

His skin had gone cold. Now he was sweating. He laughed at himself and hauled one of his feet clear to turn towards her.

'Only a bit of wood,' he called. 'Told you!'

As he climbed the bank he said, 'A piece of bog oak isn't a body.'

But she was pale. 'Let's go back,' she said. 'I don't care what it is, it's evil.'

He laughed as he tore handfuls of grass to clean the mud from his feet. 'Your imagination!' he said. 'It even gets me going at times.'

2

In the big room the sun stretched itself along the carpet.

The evening class had gathered for an end-of-term party in Mrs Knowles's house beside the river, but it was still a class, still talking literature. Mrs Knowles was trying to escape from it. She needed something more.

'I have to take things literally,' she said. 'It's no use talking theories to me.'

'But I wasn't theorizing,' objected Miss West, of the long clever face. 'All I was trying to do was bring a little intelligence to bear.'

'Feelings,' said Mrs Knowles. 'Sensations. You have to feel a poem. You can't analyse it.'

'Oh come now,' said Miss West. She sat very straight in her chair. All she had to put against the good looks and the wealth of Mrs Knowles was her intelligence. She was using it like a sword. 'If you don't bring your intelligence to bear, the result is mere sloppiness.'

There was a personal edge to what the two women were saying that kept the others silent. The teacher, Rob Dawson, was scratching a match against the box just not hard enough to light it.

'You may be right.' Mrs Knowles was smiling. It was a party. She did not want it spoiled. She leant forward until she dipped her head in the sun. Her face, even in this brightness, showed few signs of middle age. 'What does a person of sixteen think, Mr Dodds?'

Dick Dodds was caught off guard. But the sun was full on him and he was able to squint into it and hide. 'I agree with both of you,' he said. It was desperate, and weak, but it was true.

Rob Dawson laughed. He said, 'You won't get a character like Dodds to blow his cool, Mrs Knowles.'

She did not understand him and sat back in her chair, discouraged.

'Coolness is all, isn't that so, Dodds?' The teacher struck his match and bent his hooked nose over his hooked pipe and brought smoke from both.

'Oh I don't know,' said Dick. Rob Dawson was amiable, better than most, but he did not know as much about his pupils as he thought.

'But your writing, Mr Dodds.' Mrs Knowles had come forward again. 'Those brilliant essays of yours are full of feeling. You must know what I mean.'

The evening classes, now completed, had been a success

for Dick Dodds. Rob Dawson had got him to join ('Older people, Dodds. It'll stretch you a bit, but it won't do you any harm') and twice he had read out things Dick had written.

Somebody else, it was Miss West, was agreeing with Mrs Knowles about the essays, and once again he was glad that the sun in his face allowed him to squint and hide.

Suddenly Mrs Knowles was at him again. 'Mr Dodds, that river out there, is it good or bad?'

'Bad.' The muddy water was twisted in thick ropes as it rushed past the front of the big house. It cared for no man.

'You see!' Mrs Knowles had small even teeth that glinted white as she smiled. 'To a poet like Mr Dodds even things have feelings. And the river is bad, I know it to be bad.'

Miss West sighed. She was not going to get involved in an argument over whether mere things had feelings. But Mrs Knowles was launched. 'My house,' she said, 'has a good side and a bad. The river is on the dark side. Everything it contains is contaminated. I saw something it had washed up the other day, a piece of wood, but the river had made it evil.'

Her cheeks were red. She was embarrassing even herself, but she had to go on.

'And out at the back of my house,' her fingers flickered against the tall bright window, 'somewhere in the distance, there is something that when it appears always gives me hope. I don't know what it is, or even where, but sometimes in the moonlight there is something that shines silver. Away in the distance. I call it the Silver Fields.'

She fell silent. Nobody had anything to say. It was up to

the teacher. 'I like your imagery,' he said. 'Dodds here ought to write something about it. It sounds like his line of country.'

It was late when they left. As the sun had gone down behind the house, the full moon had risen like a counter-weight on the other side so that the roof-tops of the town punched out black shapes against the pale sky. The river that split the town in two came in a wide sweep almost to the foot of the big house but the water was hidden in deep shadow between its banks. The air was still hot.

Dick and Mr Dawson walked as far as the bridge together.

'Well, I enjoyed that, Dodds. Nothing like beginning the summer holiday with a bit of a party.'

'Yes.' Shyness shortened Dick's replies.

Mr Dawson's pipe glowed red near his chin. His thoughts were on the house they had just left. 'Saw how the other half live tonight,' he said. 'Shan't ever do it on a teacher's screw.'

Dick laughed with him.

'But hell's bells, Dodds, aren't the rich neurotic? Rich widows, at least.'

'No more than teachers.' His own comment caught Dick by surprise. His last word came out thinly, forced out on a strangled breath.

But Rob Dawson was laughing. '*Touché*,' he said. 'Mrs Knowles's sherry has done something for you, Dodds.'

Dick mumbled, his words clogged with embarrassment.

Mr Dawson took his pipe from his mouth and waved away Dick's apology. 'At least you've never heard your old benighted master burbling on about black rivers and silver fields. I thought something really interesting was coming out when she got on to that tack, but all of a sudden she seemed to clam up.'

'Yes.' One-word replies were safest.

They were on the bridge, the single concrete span that joined the two halves of the town like the thread of a wasp's waist. The teacher paused, obviously intending to take a route different to Dick's. 'Mind you,' he said, 'this fenland has something about it. It's got a lot to do with the way people behave.'

'I suppose so.' Dick was on the defensive. People from other places always found the fens strange and expected the people to be the same.

'However, I've grown to like it here,' said the teacher. 'In the summer, anyway.' He drew on his pipe. 'I even like the beer.'

That's what was on his mind. Across the road the door of the Falcon stood open, full of yellow light.

'Time for a couple,' he said. 'Enjoy your holiday.'

'Yes,' said Dick. 'Good night.'

3

Dick stood alone on the bridge. It was like finishing a book or coming out of the pictures and having nobody to talk to. You were left with a head full of passions in a dull world that would not respond. Too late now for the park gate; there would be nobody there. But the night demanded something yet.

At each corner of the bridge the concrete balustrade curved to make a little alcove, each with two lamps. Eight lamps palely burning, and himself the only actor on the stage. He leant on the concrete and looked over. The river ran in a narrow and deep channel through the town, filling and emptying with the tides of the distant sea. It was full now; a high tide had pushed it up so that it lay only a few feet below the level of the road alongside it. It was like a road itself, but the lamps on the bridge and along the brink shone on it. Not evil. Glamorous. Like a canal in Venice. Streets of water must look like streets after rain.

'Rain-faced Venice,' he said. Mrs Knowles would have liked the phrase, even if her dark river inspired it. But it was a phrase by itself. It led to nothing.

He sighed and stuck his hand in his hair, let it fall over his forehead and looked upwards through it at the moon. Gesture of a man alone and unobserved.

He left the bridge and walked downstream. Buildings crowded so close to the road that the pathway was cantilevered out to overhang the river, but when the centre of the town was behind him the road broadened into a wide quay. It was built on a high bank that, on the side away from the river, canted steeply down to a row of small houses. Their bedroom windows could only just see over the edge. Boats floated almost level with the roof-tops.

From the town the clock in the tower of the Institute Hall began to chime the hour. Ten o'clock, an even number. He looked back at the yellow moon-face of the clock under its pinnacle, and waited. There was a pause and then the bells began again, stumbling into a hymn tune. Every other hour, day and night, they did the same. A clear sound, shaken out mechanically, as unheeded as a bell buoy in a lonely sea.

'Ocean-going music,' he said. It pushed his mind down the river and out into the fens as he listened.

Black boats, tethered close, stood still on the surface of the water. And the dare entered his mind.

Suddenly he was panting. The heart-leap of the dare, then the qualms of the coward.

Steal a boat. No, no.

But the quay is empty, an invitation. Cast loose. To the first bend and back to prove yourself.

No, go back. The town is safe.

Safe for cowards. Full of torment for ever.

Very well. A bargain. I walk fifty paces. If there is a boat I can use I will go. If not, I am free.

Agreed.

Dick walked, counting footfalls. He passed two cruisers. Both too big. Ahead lay another. Beyond that, nothing for many yards. He came level with the third cruiser and his breathing was beginning to shudder into an easier rhythm. But there was no escape. Outboard of the cruiser, half-hidden under its flank, a small rowing boat lay waiting for him.

Act now.

He looked quickly up and down the quay. Still alone. He went to the edge. The cruiser had its fenders out and was held even further from the quay by a wide baulk of timber in the water. A couple of yards. But there were handgrips along the canopy over the cockpit and a ledge for his feet. He leapt, reaching for the grips. His feet hit the deck.

A boat is a floating drum. The thud of his feet echoed

within it and at that instant he thought of people on board. He clung, and fear stripped him as clean as a skeleton. It happened once in every real dare.

He clung. Nothing stirred. The cruiser was deserted. Stiffly he worked his way round the canopy and looked down into the boat. His breath was shallow but he did not pause. He slid down into the boat and crouched. The boat rocked and rattled its ridged sides in the water, pushing out little waves, but they were quickly erased. He remained still and his breathing, for the second time, steadied.

Triumph warmed him. His test was half over. Now to the bend and back.

The boat's painter was made fast to a cleat in the cruiser and he had to reach high to cast it off, and then again to free the stern rope. Moving quickly now, he pushed off, reached for an oar and got its blade on to the gunwale. He reached for the other. Nothing there but the shadow of the boat's side. There was only one oar in the boat.

He hauled his panic down, muttering. One oar was enough. He had seen men sculling with one, and there was a notch in the stern. He rested the oar in it, stood up and stirred the blade in the water. The boat moved. He twisted the blade as he plied it to and fro, and the boat was under control. He had discovered a talent.

Calmly now, he plotted his voyage. The cruiser was some distance away and, despite the moonlight, difficult to pick out. He needed a marker for his return and noted its position against the black roof-tops behind it. On the stern of his boat, just under the notch, he could see some carved letters and he bent to read them. 'Tender to Sea Mist.' The cruiser's name. It might help.

He looked up. A grain elevator on the opposite bank had shifted itself further upstream. The tide had begun to turn. The river swirled in little whirlpools alongside, restless but not yet properly launched on its slide down the channel to the sea.

He thrust with the oar. The houses slid behind. To the left a grassy bank rose high enough to hide the flat fields beyond, but on the right the quay stretched some distance yet. He was passing a timber yard, stacks of planks gleaming white under the moon. Further on, there were the tanks of the oil depot with a tanker alongside the jetty. Beyond it the grass came down to the edge on both sides.

Sculling tired him. He paused. He was out on the open water, vulnerable. To the tanker would be far enough.

Now that he was within his capabilities he sculled easier. The clock-face in the town was small, unreadable. Then the timber yard blotted it out. The moon was golden and fat, the river high and full; the Venetian road tempted him to travel. But the tanker loomed and he thrust his oar to turn towards it.

He cut across the river in a wide sweep, going faster than he thought, and suddenly he was in danger of ramming the ship's side. He tried to do two things at once, steering with the oar with one hand and reaching forward to fend off his bows with the other. He had to stretch too far and was amidships, spreadeagled, when his bows thudded into the cold plates. The jolt unbalanced him, and as he fell the river fastened on the blade and snatched the oar from his hand. He lay on his back and watched the shaft stagger across the sky.

He reached for it, but uselessly, and he heard it splash before he got himself upright. And then he was leaning over with the planks hard on his ribs. But it was gone, bedded in the ripples, hidden. And yards of water had opened between him and the ship.

There were lights on deck, and the portholes of the crew's quarters shone yellow. He saw somebody's head moving in a cabin. The ship's generators were thumping, and there was the faint whistle and hum of machinery. He clutched the side of the boat, and fear covered him like a rolling wave.

And then suddenly the fear slid away. He was in no danger. It was a joke.

He pushed the sleeve of his jacket up as far as it would go and dug his hand into the water. He thrust hard and fast and moved closer to the ship. He thought he saw a rope to cling to. Quickly he shifted sides to keep his bows pointed but he could not correct the swing, and the river's bloated belly gave a soft malicious heave that put him out of reach of the ship for good. Its wrinkled skin was pulsing as it began to push towards the sea.

Panting, he sat back. A cry for help? He was in no danger. There were worse things to be afraid of. He spoke loud.

'Boat-stealer, oar-thief, you have no friends!'

He calculated. The river was not yet flowing with any speed. It was likely that at the bend he would swing nearer the bank. A desperate paddle might do it. He would save himself for that. So he sat and waited as the boat meandered downstream.

At the bend, things began to go his way. The boat, his friend, slid from midstream towards the bank and even pointed its bows to help him. Kneeling in the bottom he stabbed the water with all his strength and the grass came within reach. He flung himself forward and reached out with his dripping hand. Relief was warming him. He stretched further.

Underneath him, the current found a reef of mud, boiled over it and plucked him away.

He sobbed for breath, not sure if he was crying, as he was smoothly carried downstream. The bend was behind him, the town was a hump of light in the sky and no sound reached him. To shout now, in this loneliness, would be to terrify himself. He curled up tight, clutching a thwart with his arms and legs. His mouth was against the wood, dribbling on it like a baby. It was a comfort. Despicable. He sat up.

The moon was full in his face. It swallowed him. It made distances tiny, almost as though he could reach out and grasp each bank of the river in his hands.

Tomorrow, Jim would laugh at him. 'You'll kill yourself one day, Doddsy.'

'But not tonight, Jimmy mate.'

Dick looked over the side. The river, brown with stirred mud in daylight, had a night sheen, black and pocked with eddies as it gained speed. He would not swim for the bank. The river had clung to too many men.

He was moving out into the fens. At times he could see the flat land beyond the low banks. The river ran straight. He knew there was hardly a bend in the seven miles to the marshes and the Wash.

The boat began to revolve, very slowly, and he was looking back towards the town when he saw a car's headlights. A chance. The lights were leaving the town, coming in towards the river at an angle as though they were looking for him. The road joined the river almost at this spot. He had forgotten. The lights were big and powerful. He stood up and waved his arms. The boat rocked. Even in the moonlight the beams drew a sharp line across the river and lit the far bank. But far above his head. Not even his fingertips were touched.

And he almost fell. He sat down quickly and felt sick.

The boat turned.

Somewhere in the distance a motor-cycle gathered speed, throttled down and then revved again and held its note along some straight stretch that took it out of ear-shot. Lying in bed on a summer night he had often listened to traffic far away, night travellers leaping miles in minutes. His turn to join them had come.

And next morning . . .

4

. . . he stood at the park gate.

'Thank God for the sunshine,' he said.

Jim Peters was laughing. 'I reckon you're a liar,' he said.

'No. All the way down to the sea,' said Dick. 'But it was flat calm. And then the tide turned and pushed me ashore.'

'But didn't you shout?'

'I shouted all right as I was going out to sea. But no-body heard.'

Jim, heavily built, had an unexpectedly high laugh. 'You'll kill yourself one day, Doddsy,' he said.

The park gate was a low iron field gate. Pat, sitting on it beside Jim, slapped at him. 'Shut up, Jim!' she said.

Jim was enjoying himself. 'You're pale, Doddsy. Do you reckon they're after you by now? What'll you tell the police?'

Dick yawned. He was worried. 'Can't stop yawning,' he said. 'Didn't get much sleep. It's a long walk in from the coast.'

'What time did you get back?' Jim had a way of wrinkling his forehead that even when he laughed made his grey eyes seem concerned.

'About five.'

'Poor old mate. But you're lucky the police didn't pick you up.'

Dick struggled to regain his form. 'I nipped down a ditch every time a car came.' He yawned. 'Thank God for the sun,' he said again.

'You're lucky to see it,' said Jim.

Pat shivered. 'That river,' she said. 'It makes me feel awful.'

'Feel her arm,' said Jim. 'All goose pimples.'

'Keep your hands to yourself!' She was small, she had long fair hair, and she bullied Jim. She slid off the gate and wriggled her hips to straighten her skirt. 'Coffee,' she said. 'Come on.'

'We've got to go and look for that boat, don't forget,' said Jim.

'I'm thirsty.'

They looked at Dick. He made no move to go with them.

'You've got rings under your eyes,' Pat said. 'You look terrible.'

'And I always thought she fancied you,' said Jim.

Dick managed to smile. He looked at both of them quickly and then across the park. It was a wide, flat field, ringed with trees. A piece of countryside which the town embraced but had not yet digested. No shrubs, no flower beds. It must have been fatigue that made everything seem tiny; miniature people on emerald grass, brittle trees that glittered. He clenched his jaw until it ached.

Pat saw the muscles make ridges in his cheeks. 'What?' she said.

Dick continued to look across the park. 'I hauled the boat up a good long way before I tied it up. It should still be there.'

'So you said,' said Jim.

'Then I had to plough through some mud.' He had also told them this, but they listened. 'I was aiming for about where that old lighthouse is, you know? Mud up to my knees. But there were some patches of grass and I kept to them most of the time, when I could. But then I came to a big wide expanse of mud.'

The sun put a gloss on the grass of the park. The moon had silvered the mud.

'But it wasn't too deep. Just over my shoes. I went straight across.'

He turned towards them. His face was pale but smooth. His eyes held them.

'Half-way across there was something I couldn't understand. A little hollow with a trail leading from it. Something had come out and slithered away across the mud.'

Pat and Jim stood close together. Her hand, half-hidden by her skirt, reached and clutched Jim's fingers.

'I couldn't understand it; still don't,' said Dick.

'Might have been an eel,' said Jim.

'As thick as a man?'

Pat stood very still. Jim's grin was awkward. Doddsy, he thought, you look too innocent with your eyebrows up like that. There's something crazy in you and I'm not getting mixed up in it. He broadened his grin and it seemed to work.

Dick held his eyes a moment longer and then looked down. 'All right. Coffee,' he said.

Jim, relieved, began to move away.

'Just a minute!' Pat stood where she was. 'What happened?'

'I'll tell you.' Dick turned quickly to face them. 'I stepped into that trail.'

Then he had to find words for it.

'Cemeteries,' he said. 'Like cemeteries opening up. I was amongst the dead.'

Jim looked at the lunatic. Dodds was thin, slightly above average height, but with a stoop now as if every nerve was pulling to bend him.

'I don't understand you, Doddsy.'

'I stepped into that trail and it seemed to put the moon out. Everything darkened. I went cold and stiff and then I fell. I must have done. I was on my hands and knees just a short distance away from the trail and I could feel the moon on my back.'

Pat had to escape. She spoke scornfully. 'You felt the moon?' she said. 'Moonlight isn't warm.'

'No. But I stood and looked at it a long time. I sort of moon-bathed.'

He had stood with his mud-gloved hands held away from his sides and stared face to face with the huge disc that had stooped to be level with him, its rim touching the horizon.

'And then I stepped back into the trail.'

'I don't know about you, Doddsy,' said Jim.

'I had to test it. It came again. Like a nightmare.'

And then Dick had had enough. He straightened and pushed his hands through his hair.

'What next?' said Jim, but Pat broke in.

'You're morbid! The pair of you!'

She would have left them, but Jim's hand held hers tightly.

'I kept my eyes on the moon,' said Dick. 'It seemed to dwindle but it didn't go out. Then I found I could step out of the trail.'

He smiled. One thing about him, thought Pat, he has nice teeth.

Dick said, 'Pat wants her coffee.'

The café had an upstairs room. Low tables, with cigarette burns, a carpet with holes in it, and deep, worn armchairs.

'Mucky old hole,' Pat said.

'But home,' said Dick. Today everything that was familiar was home.

They sat in the armchairs round a table. It was cool and smelt musty. There was nobody else in the room. They ordered their coffee and sat in silence except for Jim who leant forward with his hands between his knees and whistled at the floor. Their coffee came.

'I've got a theory,' said Dick.

Jim stopped whistling and looked up without moving his head. He had heard those words from Dick before.

'It might have been marsh gas or something coming out of the mud where the surface was broken. I might have breathed it and gone light-headed.'

Jim said, 'How is it things are always happening to you?'

'He makes them happen,' said Pat.

She knew how to hurt, but today he was not allowing himself to be touched. He smiled.

'Well, it's true,' she said.

'And I thought I was convincing you.'

Dick put mock pain in his voice, and she wrinkled her nose and put the tip of her tongue out at him.

Jim laughed. 'Isn't she sweet?' he said.

'She's right, though,' said Dick. 'The theory doesn't work.'

'Why?' said Jim.

'Something even stranger happened.' He heard Pat's sigh but ignored it. 'Even when I got on dry land I got the same sensations. Exactly. When I moved into certain places I went cold.' It had been worse than coldness.

'After-effects,' said Jim.

Dick shrugged. 'I don't know. But I don't think so. Whatever came out of the mud left a trail in the air.'

'That's daft!' Pat would have none of it.

Dick agreed with her. 'Yes,' he said. 'But that's why I want to go down to the coast. I don't give a damn about the boat.'

More than he intended to say. She had needled it out of him.

'Drink your coffee,' she said. She was prim now, infuriating.

Jim began to whistle. Perhaps he was thinking. Perhaps he was bored. Dick looked angry.

'What's up, Doddsy?' Hints were never enough for Jim.

'Nothing.'

'I thought you were getting wild with me.'

'No.'

Jim was satisfied. He started to whistle again. Dick drank his coffee quickly and stood up.

'See you this afternoon,' he said.

'Going?' Jim was surprised.

'Need a rest. See you.'

Down the cool stairs and out into the heat. The harsh bright shells of the parked cars, bubbles that refused to burst, made his head ache. If all the people could have been swept away he would have lain down on the hot flagstones and slept.

He lived on one of the busy roads. Traffic surged and he had to breast its din. His home was on a corner, a tall house at the end of a terrace. There was no front garden, but there was a yard through a gate at the side. The silence began there.

He held his breath until he had found the key and opened the kitchen door. A ritual to keep the town out. He shut the door, lungs aching, and gasped for air. Safe again. There was nobody at home.

It was a long climb to his bedroom. Three steep flights of stairs. It was as lonely as a lighthouse.

He began to laugh to himself, quietly. 'Stupid,' he said. 'It's all stupid.'

In his room he got the trousers he had hidden under his bed. There was still a lot of mud. He rolled them up and put them back.

There were papers and books on the table beside his

bed. This holiday he meant to write one perfect thing; no matter how short, perfect. His handwriting looked like an infant's.

'People with your sort of brilliance, Mr Dodds,' he said, and lay down.

He closed his eyes. The smell of mud. He frowned.

But you're crazy. Why did you go in that boat? Mrs Knowles, can you tell me why I went down the river in that boat? Why did you put the idea in my head, you and your dark side and light side and your Silver Fields? Silver Fields!

'No! No! No!' He writhed on the bed. 'I'm not a crank like you!'

He lay in silence for a while. 'Not like you,' he said. 'Worse.'

He yawned, and let his eyes open just wide enough to see a beam of sunshine brightening a small patch of the carpet. If he waited long enough it would come to him as silently as a burglar's footsteps. Let it.

He slept.

5

His mother called from downstairs and he woke. He felt sleazy. Sweat seemed to have gathered in every crevice. But he had been wrong about the patch of sunlight; instead of coming towards him it had moved further away. He was pleased to have been wrong. Too many things had seemed inevitable. He was cheerful when he went down.

She smiled at him. 'Fish and chips,' she said, 'as your father's not here.'

'When's he back?'

'You know very well when he's back. Tea-time.'

'Better get the fishy smell out of the kitchen before then.'

'Honestly, to hear you talk you'd think he was an ogre.'

'No, he's a commercial traveller.'

Too far, he'd gone too far. His mother was silent.

'Well, he is,' he said.

'I know he is. It's the way you said it.'

She was a small woman, dark, neat, a bustler. There was almost always something on her that glittered, huge earrings, a bright stone on her finger. But sometimes she would shed all her beads, and a bitter depression would make her haggard.

'All right,' he said, 'I didn't mean it.'

She did not look at him and he waited anxiously. But then she relented.

'And where were you last night to all hours? Some girl, I suppose.'

'Ma,' he said, and laughed, 'I got swept down the river in a boat and stuck in the mud.'

'Was she with you?'

'It's the truth. I swear it.'

'Call me Ma once more and I'll crown you.'

They were in the kitchen. They would have been in the dining-room if his father had been at home.

'There was a lovely moon last night,' she said. 'It must have been nice down by the river.'

'It was,' he said.

'Romantic.'

'You're on the wrong tack,' he said.

They were playing a game they enjoyed, telling the truth and pretending it was lies. You only believed what you wanted to believe. But suddenly she became serious. 'You weren't in a fight, were you?'

'What, at Mrs Knowles's party?'

'I suppose not.' But she was worried. 'I had a funny feeling last night,' she said, 'sitting here alone. You weren't here, Dad wasn't here. I felt frightened.'

'What of?'

'I don't know. Just very cold. I got the shivers.'

'When?'

'Oh I don't know. Very late. And then it went. I was going to sit up for you, but then I thought I'd better not be silly.'

'There's the kettle,' he said.

The electric kettle standing beside the teapot on the dresser began to boil. She jumped to her feet and began to make tea. He wanted to let her into his mind, but he did not dare.

'And if you go out tonight,' she said, 'don't be as late as last night.'

'And how late was that?'

She looked at him over her shoulder. 'Late enough.'

6

The sun was master. It devoured the cloudless sky and made the river, running low and as brown as the uncovered mud on either side, look as warm as soup. Their cycle tyres made a faint crackling sound in the hot tar of the road. They were not far past the place where he had waved uselessly at the car.

'Doddsy's quiet,' said Jim.

'So would you be,' Pat said, 'if you'd spent half the night down there.'

Dick had not expected her sympathy. 'I didn't mean to do it,' he said. 'It was forced on me.'

'I hate water,' she said.

The bank along which they rode was a green wall across the fens. The fields, black in winter, sunned their summer colours. High pylons spaced out their geometry to the horizon.

Long before they got to it they could see Fen Bridge.

'See that,' said Dick. 'That was my last chance.'

The lattice-work span of the bridge rested on a heavy column that rose from the middle of the river. It could swing on the column to let ships pass.

Dick said, 'I really thought that was going to save me. Instead, I just about,' he shrugged, 'you know.'

'Know what?' Jim had no tact.

'I almost damned well drowned.'

'How was that?'

'The boat ran straight at the pillar.' They were twenty

yards from the river but he smelt the cold, rich reek of the mud. 'I saw an iron ring, but I had to stand up to reach it and I was going fast by then.'

That was enough. Leave the rest unsaid.

Jim insisted. 'What happened?'

Slimy stonework. Still the feel of it on his fingers. His hands slid as he leant and he was falling towards the water.

'I missed the ring but the boat hit something and I was jerked back into it.'

'Lucky,' said Jim.

Not luck. It had been savage. As though the river's patience had run out. It told him, Stay there, you're mine.

They stopped in the centre of the bridge and looked at the water hugging and sucking the column.

'If you'd gone in,' said Jim, 'you know what?'

'What?'

'You'd have gone up and down with the tide for days before they found you.'

'Jim!' said Pat. 'Shut up!'

A boat was coming upstream.

Jim put wrinkles into his brow. 'Hurry up,' he told Pat. 'They're opening the bridge. Can you feel it?'

She rode in a panic to the end of the bridge while Jim cackled. 'It's only a little old boat,' he called after her. But she would not come back.

She kept shouting 'Jim, come off!' until, still laughing, he started to move towards her.

'Henpecked,' said Dick.

Jim hunched his shoulders. 'What can you do?' he said.

Dick remained where he was. Jim, standing beside Pat, shouted, 'Come on, Doddsy.'

'Just a minute.'

There were two men in the boat, both stripped to the waist, lolling back. Dick yawned. It satisfied him to see the muddy water trodden under as the boat made headway against the current. Just before it reached the shadow of the bridge he raised one hand slightly. Just as lazily, one of the men raised his hand in reply.

They had a small boat in tow. A little docile thing. Certainty tightened his jaw. He did not need to look. Very deliberately he yawned again, squeezing moisture into his eyes so that he could barely read the words in the boat's stern – 'Tender to Sea Mist'. It went beneath him out of sight and he rode slowly to the others.

'Take your time,' said Jim.

'Well, anyway,' said Dick, 'that's one thing off my mind.'

'What do you mean?'

'There goes the boat. Back where it belongs.'

Jim was startled. 'That it? True?'

Dick nodded. They all three crossed the road to watch the two boats diminishing upstream.

'You sure?' said Jim again.

Dick nodded.

Jim looked at him sharply, close to disbelief. And then he laughed. 'I've got to hand it to you, Doddsy. You're pretty cool.'

'Well, somebody had to find it.'

'I reckon you rang up and told them where to look.'

'How would I know where to ring?'

Dick was calm, but he knew this seemed suspicious. He tried to explain his calmness. 'But I'll tell you what – I was so sure it was my boat that I nearly didn't bother to stay and find out.'

''Course you had to stay!' Indignation made Pat's cheeks red.

Dick shrugged. She frowned, but said nothing. He made them ride on and after a few yards he turned off to continue towards the river mouth.

'Hi! Where are you going?' said Pat.

They were no longer on a true road. On this side of the river they were on a track along the bank. Dick stopped and looked back. He said nothing. He seemed to her to be haughty.

'You've found your boat,' she said. 'Now we're going home.'

'Hole in the mud,' said Jim. 'That's what he's really interested in.'

'That rubbish!'

Jim coaxed her. 'Come on,' he said. 'We've got to humour him now we've come this far.'

Dick was cycling on slowly, dawdling for them.

'Well, I'm not going into any mud,' she said. 'Not for him.' She glowered at his back. And she did not like cycling along the high bank. Only the fact that there was a flat strip of grassland, a berm, between the bank and the river prevented her refusing to go on.

Dick rode with his head bent forward, looking neither right nor left. It was an extravagant slump.

'I wonder what's up with him now,' said Jim. 'He'll be over the edge if he don't watch out.'

They were catching up with him.

'He's showing off,' said Pat. She pulled the corners of her mouth down.

They came alongside. Still he did not raise his head.

'Watch where you're going, Doddsy,' Jim called.

No reply. Suddenly Pat felt guilty. He had heard what she said and was offended.

'Is anything wrong?'

He always troubled her. It should have been easy to like him. She liked his looks. But he was too distant.

He said nothing. She leant forward to look into his face. Misery that was too great for any expression had smoothed it and made his eyes dead.

'I didn't mean it,' she said.

He heard nothing.

'Oh, dear!' There was panic in her voice. She stood on her pedals to lean further forward. 'Dick, I'm sorry!'

She put a hand out to him, began to lose her balance, and grabbed his arm. Together they swayed to the edge of the track, the long grass caught at their wheels and, very slowly, laid their bicycles flat. They stepped clear, sliding a pace or two down the bank and stood, side by side, facing the river across the berm.

Above them, Jim chuckled. She was holding Dick's hand. She was hot and confused.

Dick turned his head towards her. The dead marble of his eyes had come to life. His lips were smiling.

'Thanks,' he said.

'What for?' She held his hand a moment longer. His fingers were cold.

'You dragged me free.'

He helped her up the bank.

'Free of what?' she asked.

He stopped her at the edge of the track. 'Just a minute.'

Jim stood a few paces away.

'It's just about where you're standing,' Dick said. 'Can you feel anything?'

Jim shook his head. Suddenly Pat knew what had happened. 'It's that feeling you had last night. Is that it?'

Dick nodded. Some of the tension had come back into his face, and she knew he was going to test the trail again. 'Can you stand beside Jim?' he said. 'See if anything happens.'

She did not want to go but she moved forward slowly. She turned when she reached Jim. 'I didn't feel anything.'

'You sure?'

'Yes. But you scare me stiff. I want to go home.'

Dick did not answer, but he began to come towards them. His eyes looked above and beyond them as he concentrated, like a man in muddy water feeling his way with his feet.

He was still four yards from them when the trail shut its mouth on him. It was sudden. Eyes shut, mouth shut, head forward with a jerk. And his arms seemed to dwindle and be absorbed into his sides. He was a pillar that was hardly human.

They stood, watching. His head began to move, lifting a blind face towards them, and then his feet scraped the earth and like an old man, night-wandering, he came towards them. They wanted to run, began to back away, but his eyes flickered open and they stood still.

'Ah,' he said quietly. 'Bad.'

Jim had his lips pursed, whistling. Nervousness made him do it.

'It's still there,' said Dick. 'In daylight. But I got myself out that time.' He was trying to smile.

Jim watched him for a moment anxiously, but the greyness was quickly draining from Dick's face. 'That was pretty good, Doddsy,' he said. 'Do it again.'

'Anything for you, Jim.' He made as if to step back into the trail.

'No!' Pat cried out.

So she believed in it. It was more than just his imagination. A barrier, invisible but as hard as iron, stood before them in the sunshine. The world was not exactly as it seemed. Dick grinned.

'Once more,' he said, 'for proof.'

He stepped towards the place, holding himself rigid, armour-plating his sensations. As he entered he kept his head up, his eyes open.

In another room. He was in another room. And from it he looked on bright fields gone grey. He breathed winter air. I am me, he said to himself. No other thought. I am me, I am me. But the smell of the mud came to drown him. The room had no door. Panic hooked feverish fingers into the joints of his armour. He lunged and was out in the sunshine.

'You changed,' said Jim. 'You suddenly went different. I don't know how you do it, but you scare me.'

'I scare myself,' said Dick.

'I'm going home,' said Pat. No more; she could stand no more.

They went with her. There was no trace of the trail across the bridge.

They talked about it, and Jim laughed. It began to seem less real.

'I shan't embarrass you by telling anyone about it,' he said.

'You will, Peters, you will,' said Dick. But he had made up his mind; his next move would be alone.

7

It was a day made up of compartments. He roamed from one to another, satisfied with none.

His father sat in an armchair in the room at the front of the house reading a newspaper. Dark suit with shirtcuff showing and a glint of wristwatch. He made the room look like the lounge of a hotel.

'Ah, Dick.' He folded the paper and stood up smiling. His eyes were genuinely friendly, as they were with everyone.

'Father,' said Dick. Sometimes they shook hands after his father had been away a night. Dick decided not.

'Going to sit down?' His father was still politely standing, slightly taller than his son.

'Well, no, actually.' Always words like this to his father. 'I had rather a tiring night, you see. I think I'll lie down for a bit.'

His father's eyes twinkled. 'Very well, old son. You run along.'

Dick shut the door. There was a sort of luxury about his father's presence. But sometimes you had to get out.

It was hot and quiet on the stairs. Like climbing, he said to himself, in the entrails of the house. Another phrase for Mrs Knowles. On the second landing the sun slanted through a window and made the carpet as warm as a bed. He sat there, curled up, and thought.

Alone again. Best like this. That trail. It will not last for ever. My sensitivity will fade. It's like believing in magic again. Make the most of the mood.

Two steps up from the landing there was a short corridor to his bedroom. The door was open and he could see the papers on his bedside table.

'Genius!' he said and groaned.

Movements downstairs. He stood up slowly, one leg gone dead, and limped into his room. He lay down and, for the second time that day, slept.

He did not wake until evening.

'I looked into your room at tea-time,' said his mother, 'but I thought it was a shame to wake you.'

'Where's Dad?'

'He had to go out again.'

'He's never here.'

'Now don't you go criticizing him.'

'I'm not.' He yawned.

'I can see *you* won't want to be going out again to-night.' She turned away, making herself busy, as though the matter was settled.

'I reckon I will,' he said. 'A bit later on.'

'Oh no.' She spoke as if she was offended.

'Well I've got to.'

'Why? What's so important?'

He grinned. 'It's not a girl. Don't worry.'

'But I do worry, Dick. That's the trouble.'

'But why, Mum?'

'Oh I don't know. I wish it was a girl. At least I'd know. It's that feeling I had last night.'

'You're just a worrier. You know you are.'

'Maybe I am. But why do you have to go out every night?'

'I promised. I said I'd see Jim and them. I won't be late.'

'You must be careful.'

It was the way she said the word 'must' that made his skin go cold.

8

Leaving his mother was difficult. He delayed until it was almost impossible. Then he left, quickly. And, as if to punish himself, he was unprepared.

A tyre needed pumping. He did it feverishly. He tested his lights. One of his batteries was giving out. Omens. But he could not stay.

In the streets he was calmer. It was warm, comfortable, like riding a bicycle through a huge house.

People were in indoor clothes, strolling. Couples kissed in doorways as though a party had reached the sprawling stage. But he did not belong.

He crossed the bridge to the curving wall of tall house-fronts that looked in on the town. It was pierced in one place only, by a narrow arch. Into its black mouth, through the cool thickness of the wall and out into the road behind. Long gardens reached down from the houses to the road, but on the other side there was open country. He clung to the shadows of the garden walls like a soldier coming secretly from a besieged castle. The trees out in the open land held themselves still.

Then he remembered the book in his pocket. Shelley, belonging to Mrs Knowles. He would return it. But from here he could not see her house. The road divided, one arm stretching away at right-angles and, now that he knew he was coming back, he turned and rode out along it.

He stopped and looked back. The houses were very tall, battlemented with chimneys. Not a single window was lit. Useless to try to see her if she was not at home. No, now he had begun, he would go on.

'Keep an eye on me, anyway,' he said, as though she was there, at one of the dark windows, watching.

The moon, that had hung like a lamp over the town, had swung out with him and showed him the distances. A long easy curve led him away between the fields and he rode without effort. It was like being swallowed by an endless throat and he let it happen.

As the town fell behind, the road straightened and he went faster. The trees became fewer and then fell away and he was out and speeding over the flat top of the world with the air pressing into his open mouth. When he came to the river he had no fear of it. It had risen to touch the grass on either side, and lay like an ornamental waterway glazed by the moon. Fen Bridge was a decorative gate to the sea.

He slowed as he approached and stopped in the middle, caged by the ironwork. There was no traffic and the water barely whispered. He waited until he was sure of his mind.

Right.

He left the bridge and turned to go inland on the other bank of the river. It was a rough track, and he rode for some yards before he crossed the strip of grass in the centre and found what he wanted.

The trail bit into him. Cold smell of mud. But he knew it. He fought the fear, bleak eyes open, until it dragged his shoulders and slowed his legs. And then he swerved out.

'I can beat it.' He spoke to the placid river.

When the anguish faded from him he dipped into the trail again, and held to it longer. He did it again and knew he was its master.

He swerved out and bent into the trail again, stabbing it, killing the fear. And he began to laugh. It was obvious. It was plain. He was a water-diviner. Simple. Beneath him there was an underground stream. Even something less; a water main. Bits of evidence flew into his mind. The tension in his muscles was a water-diviner's cramps. This was why he feared water, and why he found it beautiful. He was attracted to it, repelled by it. Water was always magic.

Of course, of course.

Then his brain paused and he rode slower, drifting into doubt. In the boat, sitting on water, he had not felt the fear that gripped him in the mud. He had never known that fear anywhere. But did it work like that? Perhaps it was only hidden water that affected diviners. And would there be an underground stream so close to the river?

And now he doubted the trail. He edged back to the line it had taken. It was still there. There was nothing he could do but follow it.

The track divided, one leg of it going down the bank at an angle away from the river. The trail went down with it, and he followed it into the ruts made by tractor wheels along the edge of a field. The earth was baked hard and he went fast, at first keeping close to the foot of the bank but, when the track turned, he suddenly found himself heading out across the plain.

It was like going out to sea. The small sound of his tyres was like the crackle of ripples against a boat's hull. In the distance the dark, low line of an orchard made a landfall, but closer was a group of tall trees, clustered close, heads together. His path led directly to them.

Faster. A shed came nearer. A tractor stood there, its huge wheels like grasshopper legs folded to leap. He went by in a hiss of dust, rocked and swayed towards the trees and plunged into the shadows of their arms.

The trees stood where three fields joined, a no-man's-land where the grass grew long. Inside the grove he lost the rutted track. Leaves touched his face. He jerked his head. He could see no way out. He stood still and the air dithered in and out of his lungs. The leaves around him and above crawled. His grip grew fierce until the iron handlebars seemed to melt and he held nothing but the bones of his own fingers.

Then he saw a gap. But the grass clung and he could not ride. He ran. A patch of flattened grass was like a pool. He leapt and in mid-leap, as though the grave in the mud had opened below him, the fear struck. It jerked his head back like a man slain. His feet hit and stumbled, but he was moving. The gap in the trees came closer and opened for him. He was mounted and riding.

Thud after thud as his wheels hit clods of earth, bucked in hollows, ripped grass. He rode in the night like a tattered horseman, on and on over black and ragged fields with the wind in his ears like the shrieks of the dead drowning his hoofbeats.

A road crossed his track. He slewed into it, stones spitting from his wheels.

A light, far ahead. He leant forward as though to hold it in his teeth and heaved the spinning iron after him as he flew.

An open gateway. A gravelled yard. Feet and wheels made black fountains of stones and he halted before they fell.

The light was above the side door of a house. Calm and pale, it possessed the yard. He drank it.

And then the door opened.

9

White moths and small flies jittered around the light bulb. Beneath it, a girl stood in the doorway.

'Sorry.' His voice was dry, reedy.

She lowered her head and looked at him suspiciously.

'I'm sorry,' he said again.

Her eyes, alarmed, seemed to glower. Humiliation faced him.

'Didn't mean to be here,' he said. 'I was out there.' He meant to point to the road outside but his hand would not free itself from the handlebar. He looked down. The white fingers slowly unclenched. When he looked up she had opened the door wider.

'Are you lost?' She knew him; had seen him before.

'No.' If he rode long enough he would find a way back to the town.

'Oh.'

'I mean yes.' He also had seen her before. Very large dark eyes. A small round face.

'Which way did you come?' she asked.

This time he was able to point. 'It's not really a road.' But she would know that. He tried to grin. Suspicion again in her face. 'I'll go,' he said.

'I thought you were my father.' She was talking to keep him there. She did not know why. 'He's out with my mother. They should be home about now.' She was blushing.

He ought to tell her more. 'I was riding up the river,' he said. 'I thought I'd see where the track went.'

'By yourself?'

'Yes.'

Not suspicion in her eyes; almost terror. Both knew it. Neither spoke. The moths alone moved in the silent yard. Far away, a small night noise freed itself and filled the sky for a moment before it died. He knew he had to hurry.

'Can I see you tomorrow?' he said. It was a necessity.

'Yes.' For the first time she took her eyes from him, listening. A car was coming.

'Where?'

She was listening to the car. 'I don't know,' she said.

Headlight beams began to lick the rough face of the hedge across the road.

Dick said, 'I'll ride out tomorrow afternoon. See you halfway.'

She nodded.

The lights bit deeper into the hedge. He moved to let the

44

car into the yard. Close to her, he was much taller. He did not want to meet her parents. He bit his lips, ready to speak to strangers, but the car did not turn into the yard. Slowly it went past the open gate.

'See you.' He was whispering.

'Good-bye.' She willed him to make haste.

He left the yard. From a garage behind an outbuilding the car's engine murmured and died. A door opened and shut, but behind him now, receding.

Dick kicked at the pedals, let himself weave in the empty road. She was very pretty.

Then suddenly he slowed, almost stopped. Her name. He did not know her name.

He started to laugh. He was still laughing when he came to the village. He did not know the name of that either.

10

He had forgotten what she looked like. A map gave him the name of her village, but he mentioned her to nobody. He went out early, in the heat of the afternoon, chasing a face he had forgotten.

He was more than half-way to her village when he stopped. The lane ahead was long and straight. Not the only route she could take but the most direct. A heap of road-mender's sand, hardened by rain and sun, made an orange hillock on the verge. He climbed it to look out over the flat land. In the distance cars flashed like a carnival in the

45

sunlight, but their sound did not reach him. If she had taken that road he had missed her.

He saw the spire of her village pricking up through a cushion of trees, still a long way off, and then he let the whole landscape rest in his eyes, and waited.

She came, no bigger than a fly, towards the end of the lane, drifting, half-hidden by hedges. He jumped down and rode towards the lane's mouth. She turned into it, a pale dress, like somebody coming through a door. When she saw him her head dipped.

Still far apart. A double black line where cars had pressed pebbles into the tar lay between them. They rode on opposite tracks. He made it an omen. They could never meet. But the distance halved and shrank and they came to rest with their feet on the pebbles.

He heard the tiny sound her lips made when they parted.

They said hello.

'Hot,' he said.

She nodded. She had dark hair, almost black. She could not be perfect, nobody was perfect. Too real. She blushed and obliterated his hazy night picture of her.

'Which way should we go?' he said. He could not remember why they were meeting.

'I don't mind.'

They stood where they were. He gripped the handle bars and felt them slide in the sweat of his palms. And then he remembered.

'Hope I didn't scare you last night,' he said.

'No. I thought you were my father coming home.'

'Sorry.'

They were tied tight in the words of the night before.

46

Still trapped, he said, 'I got lost.' He felt his lips curl. Say anything. 'I don't know your name.'

'Why not?' Not what she meant. They were speaking like angry strangers.

'Helen Johnson.'

Her name, public property. Her eyes were on him. He expected her to ask his name, and opened his mouth to answer, but she said, 'I know yours.'

'How?'

'Pat Patterson told me.'

'When?'

'Ages ago.'

'Didn't know you knew her.'

'Sort of.'

The spurt of words ended. He had to tell her how he had blundered into her yard.

'Shall I show you where I got lost last night?' he said.

'All right.'

They rode side by side back the way she had come. Just before they reached the end of the lane she drew in her breath as though she was about to speak and he turned towards her quickly, but her eyes flickered away and she said nothing. He waited, and when she spoke he kept his eyes away from her.

She said, 'I know where you went last night. Did you see anything?'

'What sort of thing?'

'You looked a bit scared,' she said.

'Did I?' He felt ashamed.

'I don't blame you,' she said. 'Out there.'

He shrugged.

She paused before she spoke again. 'I saw something,'

she said. His head jerked round. 'Not last night,' she said. 'The night before.'

'Stop!' Their feet scraped the road. She looked up at him. Tawny man; hair, eyebrows, eyes. 'Tell me,' he said.

'My dad's got a shed at end of the drove through those orchards where you were last night,' she said. 'I had to go there because I'd left a book. I was inside and I looked out. You know there's some tall trees.' He nodded. 'I was looking through the window and I thought I saw something move just by them. It's a mucky old window so I wiped it.' She made a quick little movement with her fingertips, making a peephole. 'It was pretty dark.'

'But there was a moon,' he said.

'Yes, there was a moon. I could just see something. A sort of shape. Just a black thing moving. I couldn't really see it.'

She was frowning slightly.

'I think it was like a man,' she said.

'Was it a man?'

'It was like a man all tied up, no legs and no arms. But it kept moving. Sort of gliding, and . . .' She did not want to go on.

'What?' He waited to be told.

'It kept falling over!'

He saw it, like a worm, writhing.

'Horrible!' she said. 'It was swaying and gliding and then falling and all I could see was this thing in the grass. But I could hardly see it and I didn't think it was there. And then it was up and swaying again.'

She stopped. He raised his eyebrows. She could see amber flecks in his eyes. They wanted to know all.

'I ran,' she said.

48

He was asking no more questions. They had entered each other's territory.

'My father went to look but there wasn't anything there. He said it was imagination. It must have been.'

Now it was necessary to tell her what he knew, but he delayed.

'Show me exactly where,' he said.

'All right.'

They left the lane. Out on the plain the air was burning. Her village lay like a sleeping dog in its hump of trees.

They said little as they approached. By the churchyard wall a red double-decker bus had nudged itself under the trees. The driver and conductor were leaning against it, their caps pushed back, squinting in the sun. The driver grinned at her and called out, with mock politeness, 'Good afternoon, Miss Johnson!' He lifted his cap.

'Hello, Billy,' she said.

He grinned after them as they went by.

'That's Billy Meekins,' she said. 'He's a devil.'

'Is he?'

'He's got two women but I don't know which one he's married to.'

No reply to that. Dick grinned, but without the confidence of Billy Meekins. He was a stranger.

They went through the village, but when the main road turned to go towards Fen Bridge she took him straight on along a narrow road with a ditch on either side. It got narrower and rougher and he recognized where they were. Ahead, on the left, a black slate roof showed above an orchard.

'Is that your house?' he asked. It seemed smaller than the night before.

She nodded.

There was a skimpy garden in front in which two thin shrubs were squeezed between a wooden fence and a bay window. It was like a house taken from a town street and needing neighbours. The front door was painted a brownish purple and in gilt letters on the fanlight there was the name Colleen.

'Colleen?' said Dick.

'What?' She was puzzled.

'The name of your house.'

'It's not. It's called Drove's End.'

He pointed at the fanlight. She was nervous and glad to be able to laugh. 'That's nothing,' she said. 'Look at this.'

The gate into the yard still stood open, and it had a metal plate with another name in raised letters, Ferndale.

'And it's really called Drove's End,' she said.

They were laughing when the side door opened.

'What's amusing you two then?' Her mother came straight into the conversation.

'All our names,' Helen said. 'Drove's End and that.'

'You mean Pear Tree House.' Mrs Johnson had hair blacker than her daughter's but her eyes were blue.

'Not another one,' said Dick.

'That's what we called it when we were first married,' she said. She wore a bright yellow blouse and blue jeans. Her smile was taunting, daring him to be shy. It was her daughter who blushed, introducing him.

'Saw you last night,' said Mrs Johnson.

'You didn't!' Helen was shocked.

Her mother was putting on the thick old glove she had taken off to shake hands. 'You should turn your boy friends out earlier if you don't want to be found out.'

'You saw him, and you didn't say!'

'Neither did you.' Mrs Johnson was enjoying herself.

'I was only in the yard,' said Dick. It sounded guilty and Mrs Johnson was amused.

'He was!' said Helen. 'He turned into it by mistake.'

'I believe you. Thousands wouldn't.'

'Oh you!' Helen turned to Dick. 'Don't pay any attention to her.'

'Be good,' said Mrs Johnson. As quickly as she had appeared she left the yard, going between outbuildings into the orchard behind the house.

They leant their bicycles against the gate. Helen was still blushing.

'Does she know what you saw the other night?' Dick asked.

'I told her. But that sort of thing doesn't sink in.'

They were silent for a moment, and then he pointed to one of the sheds. 'Is that where you were when you saw it?'

'No, further up the drove.'

She led him out through the gate. Dick felt happy. Meeting her mother had been too sudden to be agonizing. The drove lay between orchards. The trees, pruned low, spread out to touch the grass on either side and made a green valley for them. He had fled down it in darkness the night before. It did not feel like the same place.

II

She walked into the long grass at the verge and reached up for a green apple. It was too high, and Dick had to drag it from the dark leaves.

He gave it to her and said, 'Like the garden of Eden. Except you should be handing it to me.'

Her mother's mischief came out. 'You don't want to get none of them ideas,' she said.

'I'm not Billy Meekins.'

'Worse.'

He got an apple for himself.

'Spit on it. They've been sprayed,' she said.

They walked, eating. There was space in the green lane but the trees seemed always to be pushing them closer. Once, they touched. She looked up at him, sideways. Dark eyes and the curve of her cheeks. He drew away, but too sharply. Confused, he hurled the core of his apple high over the trees.

'Hope it didn't hit my father,' she said.

'Eh?' His mouth was open and she laughed.

'Don't worry. He's right down the far end.'

He listened and thought he heard voices, but far off, mumbling like bees in thick grass. Ahead of them, where the trough of trees ended, a hut was squeezed into the corner of an orchard.

'Is that it?' he asked.

She nodded. There was a small open space in front of it, and the door stood open.

'Better see if anybody's inside,' she said.

He went with her to the door, but the shed was empty.

'Nice place for reading,' he said.

She was startled. 'How did you know I came here for that?' she said.

'You told me you'd left a book.'

'Oh yes.'

He followed her inside out of the sharp heat of the sun. It was stifling. He saw in the dust of the window the patch her fingers had cleared. He went to it and looked through. Peephole into something he had almost forgotten. Along the edge of the orchard, the track and the tall trees.

He clenched his teeth until the blood hummed in his ears. Her voice came to him thinly.

'That way,' she said. 'It came straight to me along there.'

Slowly, he straightened. 'Both of us,' he said. 'You and me.' But he was mumbling, hiding his words.

'What?' she said. She had gone pale.

'I came along there last night,' he said.

His breath was shallow and he did not trust himself to say more. But he led the way outside and in the sudden stab of the sun he said, 'Let's go and see.'

He walked quickly, leaving her a pace behind, deliberately. If the trail was there, he had to find it first. Near the place he made her stand still and went on alone.

It was there, a grey, cold corridor. It chilled his skin as though rain had bitten through his shirt, and it put a haze over the sky. But he saw, only a pace from him, the burnished stems of feather-headed grass gleaming in the sun.

He stepped through and turned for Helen. She was still

between the orchards. He was out in the open, beyond the edge of the matted apple trees.

She came towards him slowly. He watched. It was an experiment on her. He had no right. But he waited. His eyes were on hers. A flicker in them, no more, and she was through.

'Someone just walked over my grave,' she said.

'You felt it then?'

She did not know what he meant. He had tested her, now she was searching into him. He began to speak and it seemed like words without meaning.

He stopped half-way. 'It's madness,' he said.

'No!' Her lips remained slightly parted.

He continued to speak. The words came, and more and more his experiences began to fit in with hers. Far behind them the bank of the river raised a wall that hid all the land beyond. In front of them was the orchard wall. They were in a vast room, but their heads moved against the blue sky and they were gigantic.

The pattern locked tight. She asked no questions. Alone, she moved towards the trail and stood where she knew it to be. She turned to face him.

'Anything?' he said.

'I don't know,' she said. She wanted to believe. 'I can't tell.' He came close. She saw the shadow that she could not feel in his eyes. She was out of it; a failure. He snatched at her hand and drew her clear.

'Come with me.' He was moving towards the tall trees. He began to run and she followed, but at the edge of the glade he slowed. Inside it, the air, though slotted with sunshine, was dank. As he walked into it, flies settled on the back of his shirt. She hung back.

'Look.' He pointed to the centre. The grass there was pressed flat. It looked wet. Flies feasted there.

She wanted to turn and go, but she saw him hesitate and then step towards the patch and she put her hand on his arm and pulled him back.

'No. It's me,' she said.

She went past him and walked quickly on to the wet grass. Flies flew in a mist and she put her hands to her head and screamed.

And then she was quivering against him. He had pulled her clear.

'Horrible!' she said. 'Horrible!' And the word was in her wide eyes also.

Beyond her he saw dust rise like smoke where a tractor turned from the orchards and began to come up the track towards them. He drew her to the edge of the glade where they stood among the low branches, not hiding but half-unseen. The tractor moved fast. Within seconds it was at the entrance to the glade and then, throttling down, inside.

He knew who the driver was. He had seen the same solemn profile beside Helen's mother in the car. A silent man. He drove past without seeing them, spun the wheel and accelerated away along the track towards the river. The noise of the engine faded.

'It's you and me, then,' said Dick. 'Your father can't help us.'

Her father had driven slowly over the centre of the glade and had noticed nothing. Without moving they looked towards the flattened grass where some miserable thing had rested in the dark.

'What can it be?' she said. 'Oh, Dick, I'm frightened.'

First time she had called him by his name. 'Don't know,' he said, 'but you get used to it.'

'I've never felt so terrible.'

He went with her into the sunshine.

'Do you want to find out what it is?' He spoke flatly, letting her make up her own mind.

There was a pause before she answered.

'We've got to,' she said. 'You won't stop until you do.'

'Would you?'

'I don't know.' But the heat was burning up her fears. 'I screamed in there, didn't I?' she said.

He laughed. 'Just a bit,' he said.

'I won't do it any more.'

They came to the shed. She bit her lip. 'I haven't tried to pick up the trail again,' she said.

He found it, running along the edge of her father's orchard. While he stood clear she went forward to dip into it, but hesitated and reached for his hand. Then she went forward. Her grip tightened and he felt her shudder.

She stepped back. 'I feel it now,' she said. She was smiling.

'I knew you would.'

The orchard joined a field of strawberries, and they walked between the rows, just clear of the trees.

'What if we come across it?' she said.

'It,' he said. 'It ... it ... it. Whatever it is. No, not a chance. It hides in the day.'

'How do you know?'

'Can't be sure of anything,' he said. 'Just guessing.'

'You don't seem bothered.'

'I ain't.' Then he said, 'Tell you what; we'd be better off if we had our bikes. Can't go walking across fields all day.' He stopped and pointed ahead. 'There must be a road that goes across there.'

'Yes,' she said.

'Well why don't we get our bikes and ride round?'

It would be safer. She thought it was a good idea.

'This way,' she said, and led him into the orchard.

It was silent under the roof of glossy leaves. The earth, ploughed and harrowed to keep down weeds, was powdery and muffled their footfalls. Long corridors of trees stretched away on either side. Once, at the distant end of an avenue, they saw people working but crossed it unseen. They penetrated deeper. She dipped under the low branches and he pursued her. She moved quickly and once she had to wait for him to catch up.

'Not far now,' she said.

They came to her house from the rear. The trees touched the outbuildings and through the slot between two sheds they saw a corner of the yard, as brightly lit as a stage. The tractor stood there, in the sun, and her father was beside it.

They heard her mother's voice. She told him she had made a pot of tea. He said, 'Is Helen there?'

Her mother came and stood by him. 'What do you think?' she said.

'What am I supposed to think?' said Mr Johnson.

'She's with her young man. You won't see much of her today.'

They saw Mrs Johnson grin. Her husband grunted and she taunted him. 'I don't blame her. She does all right for herself, I'd say.'

'He sounds like a rum 'un to me.'

So he had been talked about.

Mrs Johnson laughed. They moved away. The stage was empty.

Shame burnt and sang in Helen. Her feverish eyes could not look at him. When he moved she knew he was leaving. But he was closer. His face was pale.

'I'm sorry,' she said.

'What for?'

'Because . . .'

No words. Their eyes were startled as their faces drew closer.

Her lips were very soft. His arm went around her waist, but she held herself stiffly and doubt clanged in his head.

Then he saw her eyes close and felt her hands press against his back.

12

They had to go through the village and they did not want to. It was exposure and they were secret. So they rode quickly, keeping themselves apart, never touching, and when they were outside they rode faster.

But the kiss was still blazing in them.

Dick stood on his pedals and shouted. Helen laughed and blushed.

'The trail!' he shouted. 'I don't give a damn about any old trail!'

He swept his arm wide. 'It's all nonsense! What is it to do with you? What is it to do with me? Nothing!'

They were expanding after the cramps of a nightmare,

and when they came to the lane where they expected the trail to cross they rode along it without stopping.

'Was that it?' said Helen.

'May have been.'

'Don't you want to follow it any more?'

'I'll tell you something,' he said. 'That trail's inside us. We can make it exist wherever we want.'

She knew it was true. She had felt nothing until he persuaded her. But there was one thing unexplained.

'What about that thing I saw?'

'Some poor old drunk.'

The last cloud in their minds shrivelled and vanished.

'Look how far you can see,' he said.

The orchards were behind them and the plain thrust out ahead, bare except for one tiny distant house which it tolerated like a small animal on its back.

'Isn't it smooth?' she said. 'I'd like to ride across it all day.'

'Then we will,' he said.

They went out over the flat land, knowing they dwindled until they were unseen, but still he saw the haze of soft hair on her arms.

When it was necessary to find a purpose they headed for the town. Its tall gasometer stood like a grey, square monument on the horizon.

'We'll see if we can find somebody,' he said.

'Who?' She was shy.

'Pat,' he said. 'You know her.'

But they rode slowly.

After a while he said, 'I don't see why they say the sun beats down. It's more like a great object leaning on you.' Another phrase for Mrs Knowles.

Mrs Knowles. She was in his mind and wouldn't leave it.

Cars went by, all their windows open, and seemed to drift clear of the ground as their wheels dissolved in the shimmer from the tarmac. The town came closer, reaching out for them, but once it had them surrounded it sagged in hot and listless streets. At the park gate two figures lolled in the green shade looking out across the grass where a few groups in summer dresses lay motionless.

They came to the gate slowly, almost silently, and neither Jim nor Pat was aware of them until Dick spoke.

'Me old mate,' said Jim, turning round. Then, surprised to see her, he said to Helen, 'Good afternoon.'

'Isn't he polite?' said Pat. Her wide mouth grinned. She was eager to know why they were together. 'Mm,' she said, 'this is a surprise!'

She was embarrassing them, and Jim, seeing this, laughed and puckered his forehead, waiting for their reply to entertain him. They said nothing, but Pat could not be put down.

'And when did you two meet?' she said.

'At midnight,' said Dick. Indiscretion was sometimes the best defence.

Pat had every mannerism of the born gossip. 'Mm,' she said again. 'Romantic.' Deliberately she left a gap for him to fill.

'By chance,' he said. This sounded more romantic than ever, and he had wanted to be casual. 'I rode into her yard last night by mistake. That's all.'

Jim was greatly amused, and seemed about to interrupt.

'Jim, shut up!' Pat knew he would spoil it.

Dick was off-balance. 'I was following that trail again,' he said, 'and took a wrong turning.' The trail. He thought he had finished with it. 'Well,' he said, 'I didn't have anything else to do because you two weren't about. Where were you, anyway?'

As an attempt to change the conversation it was too weak.

'Never you mind,' said Pat.

Jim spoke to Helen. 'He's told you about the trail, then?' he said.

Dick, to protect her, had not looked at her while he was answering questions. Now he did so. Her head was slightly lowered and she was looking at Jim with suspicion.

'Yes,' she said. Only one word, but her eyes, shy and defiant, stayed on Jim until he reddened.

'See,' said Pat, 'being nosy will get you nowhere.' A master stroke from the most inquisitive of them all, and Dick laughed.

But Jim spoke to Helen. 'You want to watch him,' he said, 'he's a bit of a nut. A very vivid imagination.'

'I feel the trail, too.'

Dick's heart leapt. In the middle of all this she was standing firm. Her head was down, like a little bull. She believed in the trail.

'We've been following it today,' he said. He even moved half a pace so he was standing shoulder to shoulder with her.

For Pat, the trail had become a bore. The questioning had to come from Jim. 'What is it, then, Doddsy?' he said.

'No idea,' said Dick.

'Well, what caused it?'

Dick, opening his mouth to speak, glanced at Helen. Her eyes were as intense as words. She forbade him to tell what she had seen.

'How do I know what it is?' he said. 'I've got an open mind. Just this feeling we get. The shivers. Something like water-divining, perhaps.'

He was covering up, but suddenly Pat was interested.

'Just a minute!' she said. 'I've got an idea.'

'This is it,' said Jim, but she ignored him.

'I know a woman,' she said, 'who feels like you do. I knew there was something you reminded me of. She sort of trembles, just like you do. *She*'s a water-diviner!'

She had solved everything. She waited to be congratulated.

'I've already thought of that,' said Dick. 'It doesn't work.'

But Pat was not to be contradicted.

'But I know her,' she said. 'And I don't care what you say, you *are* water-diviners. And to prove it I'm going to take you there right now.'

13

They did not have far to go. Behind the trees at one corner of the park little roads and small houses nudged right up under the branches. It was a town within a town. Pat led them in, and the red brick walls of the houses closed around them, deadening sound. They turned two corners and were cut off.

A short straight street lay ahead of them. 'Here we are,' said Pat.

'But this is where you live,' said Jim.

'So does Mrs Shepherd.'

The houses, all joined together, were like a bank riddled with rabbit holes. Between every pair of doors an arched tunnel led through to the back. Tiny patches of garden, many with broken fences and the earth trodden to dust, edged the road. On one doorstep a group of children sat silently.

Pat was chattering. 'Mrs Shepherd's a real diviner, you know. Ever so good at it. People pay her to do it.'

'I can't breathe,' said Helen.

'Just like being in an oven,' said Dick.

The four drifted to a stop and left their bicycles at the kerb. The children watched them. 'Hello,' said Pat, smiling at them like a little mother, but they did not even blink. 'Kids,' she said, 'they're all the same.'

They were close to one of the tunnels. It gaped at them with a wedge of sunlight in its mouth. Pat went into it, and they could just see that it continued behind the houses as a path between tall wooden fences. There was a gate in each fence. Pat stopped at the one on the left and rattled the latch.

'I hope she's in,' she said.

The others were still in the shadow of the tunnel. It was almost cold. Helen shuddered. She wanted to get out.

'See if it's open, Pat,' said Jim.

'She always bolts it, I know,' said Pat, but she tried the gate and it opened. She went through, giggling, and called out sweetly, 'Mrs Shepherd!'

Jim went with her, and Dick and Helen followed

quickly, anything to get out of the tunnel to somewhere they could raise their arms.

They were in a narrow yard at the side of the house. They looked down it to a long strip of garden and beyond this to another row of houses, buttressed at regular intervals by the grey slate roofs of lean-to sculleries. Between the two rows of houses the gardens were like the tangled greenery in a dried-up moat. There seemed to be no air.

Pat knocked at the back door. There was a muffled sound inside. Helen felt the skin of her arms roughen. She wanted to go, anywhere where the horizon did not rise above her thick with chimney-pots.

'Hello, Pat.'

The woman at the door was small, plump, white-haired. She was smiling. She had a friendly face.

Pat spoke like a housewife popping in to see a neighbour. 'Hello, Mrs Shepherd. I hope we haven't disturbed you.'

'No, my dear. I was just going upstairs for my rest. So you caught me just right.'

Pat apologised, profusely, while Mrs Shepherd looked at them one by one through her metal-rimmed spectacles and bobbed her head at each. Pat was getting to the point of their visit when Mrs Shepherd interrupted.

'I don't know what you're all standing out there for,' she said. 'Come on in.'

The kitchen was dim and small and smelt of cooking. In a dark corner there was another door. They went through, barely able to see anything, following the line of chatter that Pat spun as she went. In the living-room there was only one window, facing the yard, but a glimpse of the garden was reflected in a huge mirror over an immense sideboard. There was a jungle of dark furniture, around which Mrs Shepherd waddled offering them biscuits from a tin painted like a Chinese pagoda. And Pat got to the point.

Mrs Shepherd beamed and nodded and then said, 'Now then, Pat, what have you all come to see me for?'

'Mrs Shepherd! I've just been telling you!' Pat was laughing, and Mrs Shepherd put a hand on Pat's knee and laughed with her.

'It's the surprise of seeing so many people,' she said. 'Now you just tell me again and I'll listen.'

With dry biscuit in his mouth, Dick tried to speak and choked. But it stopped Pat. She had said too much before. His voice was strangled, limiting his own words. 'We wondered if we were water-diviners,' he said.

'Yes,' Pat began, 'you see they've been having all sorts of strange . . .'

Dick let himself cough, but he need not have bothered. Mrs Shepherd was paying little attention to Pat.

'I thought so,' she said. Her eyes were on him. 'I can tell.' She had silenced them and she enjoyed her power. Her eyes held Dick's for a moment longer and then switched to Helen. 'And another one if I'm not mistaken.'

She turned from them and, with the pressure of her bright black eyes no longer holding him, Dick glanced at Helen. She was afraid.

Mrs Shepherd went to a tall old dresser of black wood, too big for the room but tamed a little by the china figures she had crowded on its shelves. She reached behind a flowered vase and took out a thin forked twig.

'My switch,' she said. She held it by one end, and the far

65

tip sprang and quivered like a skinny arm. 'It's all right, dear,' she said.

She seemed to be talking to the switch, soothing it, and Dick drew in his breath sharply. Then he saw she was looking at Helen who was very pale.

'It's not doing anything at the moment,' said Mrs Shepherd. 'It can't till I hold it right. Now watch.'

She held the twig in a curious way with the thin ends trapped in her knuckles and the fork pointing away from her. She had strong forearms and they saw the muscles bunch suddenly as though she was struggling to hold a great weight. And the tip of the twig lunged away from her and dipped to quiver at the table-top as though it longed to kiss its own reflection with a tiny mouth.

Helen cried out.

For what seemed to Dick to be a vindictive moment, Mrs Shepherd stood still before she released one wing of her thin bird and turned to Helen.

'There's water under this house, my dear, and it's me that feels it, not the twig.' It sprang up and down in her hand. 'I don't even have to have a twig. A bit of copper wire will do.'

Helen sat with her hands in her lap and said nothing, but Pat said, 'Oh, Mrs Shepherd, it makes me feel funny.'

'You're a funny thing anyway,' said Mrs Shepherd, chuckling. 'But never mind that. On your feet, everybody. Outside into the sunshine.'

They went with her into the yard and stood around her as she smiled up at them. She was very small and plump.

'You're pale, child,' she said to Helen. 'Give me your hand.' She gave the twig to Jim and enclosed the hand Helen held out in both of hers. 'There now. If you have the gift it will do you nothing but good. Nothing but good, do you understand me?' Helen was beginning to feel the warmth of the sun. 'There now,' said Mrs Shepherd again, 'you're getting some colour back into your cheeks.'

She released Helen's hand and turned to Jim. 'Give it me, boy,' she said, and took the switch. 'Now look,' she said to Helen, 'you hold it like this.' The thin twig was between her fingers so that two knuckles on each hand were in front of it, and two behind. 'But not too tight or it'll take the skin off you.'

Helen's confidence was returning. The twig was beautiful, a pale and polished amber. She took it, and Mrs Shepherd helped her lace it between her fingers and then stepped back.

Helen stood alone, her hands grasping the twig, the fork pointing straight ahead, and for the first time that afternoon she was in control.

'There's no water just here,' said Mrs Shepherd.

Helen knew.

'Try walking around. You're quite safe, dear. Just get the feel of it.'

She went slowly down the yard. She heard the others moving behind her.

'Not too tight, now,' said Mrs Shepherd.

Helen's knuckles were white, She eased the pressure.

'That's lovely.'

And Helen was happy. Dick moved up beside her. They were going somewhere, clear and away together.

A fraction of a second, a splinter of time before the twig tip moved, his bare arm came close to hers. They did not touch but her arm felt a feather of air. It was like a touch

67

of metal. Her arm sang with the jar of it. And the twig twisted its beak up and back to reach her.

'Step back!'

Mrs Shepherd's voice rang in her head and the twig writhed, down and away as though to get free. She fought it, hauled it back from the spot where it wanted to stay.

Suddenly it ceased to move. Hard in her fingers, no limpness in it, but still.

Helen's eyes were bright and her cheeks were flushed. Mrs Shepherd held the fork and slowly Helen's grip eased.

The old woman was beaming. 'I played a little trick.' She patted Helen's hand. 'Look.' She pointed at a round manhole cover a few paces from them. 'That's my rain-water cistern.'

The jerking twig had frightened Pat, but now she was laughing. 'All the houses along here have got a cistern like that,' she said. 'I ought to have known. Oh dear.'

'My hands!' said Helen. There were red marks on her fingers as though the twig had lashed her.

Mrs Shepherd silenced them. 'Now I've got one more thing to tell you,' she said. She raised her hand with the switch. 'Never show off. I mean it.' Her round face was stern. 'You've got a gift and there's people who'd ask you to do bad things with it. Pay them no heed. Never ever.'

'Can I have a go now?' said Jim.

'There's no point. Only these two have got the gift.'

'Give it to Dick, then.' Jim was rarely angry, but he raised his voice.

'Don't take on.' Mrs Shepherd faced him. 'You're a good friend, that I know, and better than this one in some ways.' She jerked the twig towards Dick. 'But it won't work for you. And I'll tell you something; he's not going to try either. He'd take it too far, like he does everything else. Am I right?'

Jim's good humour was restored. His grin was wide.

'No,' said Mrs Shepherd, 'it's just for this little girl here. She's sweet, and she needs somebody on her side.'

Helen was looking at the ground.

'There now,' said Mrs Shepherd. 'I've said my piece. Now would you all like to come in again?'

But Pat said no, they had to go, and 'you know you need your rest, Mrs Shepherd'.

'Well, that's true, my dear, especially after this. Divining takes it out of you, doesn't it?'

Helen nodded. Her arms and shoulders ached. They said good-bye as they moved towards the gate, but Mrs Shepherd did not answer. She stood still, thinking, and they paused. Then her eyes became sharp again.

'I know just how you feel, my dear,' she said. 'But just imagine what it's like for someone my age.' She took Helen's arm so that Helen could help her indoors, but when Pat began to fuss around her she brushed her away. 'I don't need two of you,' she said.

Mrs Shepherd and Helen went in together.

In the heat of the yard, Dick was cold. Jim looked at him. 'She don't like you all that much, Doddsy,' he said.

'Reckon not,' said Dick.

14

So it was over. The big adventure had dwindled. They lay on the grass in the park, making their own island in a flat green sea.

'So you're water-diviners,' said Pat. 'Isn't it marvellous?'

'Yes,' said Helen. It was left to her to respond to Pat's excitement. Dick had been silent since they left Mrs Shepherd.

Pat lay flat, looking at the sky. She had her shoes off and Jim was lacing blades of grass in her toes.

'Who's doing that?' she said.

'Dick.'

'No it's not. Leave off.'

The grass was warm under Dick's shoulders and head. Only a water-diviner. It was like a new party trick; a trick, and he had turned it into a destiny. He winced and opened his eyes. Deep in the blue a swallow swam and vanished. He pressed his arms along the grass, spread-eagled. He pressed and the whole park seemed to tilt, turning and turning until he had the falling world at his back and was looking down into the depths of the sky. His heart fluttered.

Jim's voice said, 'What are we doing tonight?'

Dick closed his eyes and sweat stood like tears in the corners. 'Don't know,' he said.

'Well, you don't have to go chasing the trail any more,' said Jim.

'I knew I was right about that.' Pat could not congratulate herself enough.

Dick wanted to get away, be alone. He jerked himself up on one elbow. Helen lay with her eyes closed. She would look like that asleep. Beyond her the grass stretched away as smooth as a green cloth. From the gate hidden in its cave of trees, little figures emerged and drifted along the path like moving models. He only had to wait long enough and the same figures would come out again. Then one detached itself.

'It's old Rob Dawson,' he said.

Jim raised his head awkwardly. 'Look at all your double chins,' said Pat, but Jim ignored her. 'He's coming here,' he said.

The girls saw a man in shirt-sleeves cycling over the grass towards them.

'Who is it?' said Pat.

'Rob Dawson,' said Dick. 'He's a teacher.'

Jim said, 'What have you been up to now, Doddsy?'

The teacher, perched high on two wheels, was embarrassed as he approached. They lay and watched him.

In his shirt-sleeves, Mr Dawson looked thinner. His smile was shy.

''Afternoon,' he said, 'Dodds ... Peters.' He gave a quick nod to each of the girls. 'No need to get up, Dodds.'

Dick, half-way to his feet, subsided, felt too awkward reclining, and stood up.

'Sorry to disturb you,' said the teacher, 'but it's a bit of luck seeing you. Just been talking about you, as a matter of fact.'

'Aha,' said Jim at Dick's feet.

'Nothing to his discredit, Peters.'

'That's a change,' said Jim.

Mr Dawson's laughter was louder than it need have been. 'Peters's wit still sparkles, I see.'

'He does his best,' said Dick.

'I've just been with Mrs Knowles,' said the teacher. 'She tells me you have a book of hers.'

The Shelley. Dick nodded.

'Well, if you could let her have it. I think she needs it.'

Something turned over in Dick's mind. A whole hidden world he no longer wanted to see. He must have nodded again because Mr Dawson went on, 'She's at home now. Providential, meeting you like this.'

'I'll take it to her,' said Dick.

'Good man.' Mr Dawson lifted his bicycle round. 'Glad to have met you,' he said to the girls, and rode off.

Jim called after him, 'Hope the parkie doesn't see you riding on the grass.'

The teacher grinned over his shoulder and kept riding.

'What an example,' Jim said.

Dick remained standing. His head was down, shoulders hunched. 'Providential!' he said. 'A tiny little coincidence and he goes and makes it an act of fate.'

Jim, squinting against the sun, looked up. 'What's bothering you now, Doddsy?'

'Nothing.' But he pushed a hand through his hair, frowning. 'Why won't they ever let you alone! I thought water-divining was the end of it and now he comes out of his way to drag me into somebody else's stupid business!'

'What's this got to do with water-divining?' said Jim.

Dick, without answering, went to pick up his bike. 'Anybody coming?'

'Not me.' Jim let his head fall on to Pat's lap.

Helen stood up. 'I will,' she said.

They left the park.

'I couldn't stay there and play gooseberry,' she said, but the other two were already out of Dick's head.

'I've got the book,' he said. 'It's been in my saddlebag for days.' Then he threw his head back. 'Oh the heat, the heat! It gives me a headache.'

The town was gasping through the afternoon, every door and every window open.

'Dick.' She wanted to ask what was troubling him, but he was frowning. She changed her mind. 'Do you know what Mrs Shepherd told me when I was alone with her?'

'No.'

'She said there were some people in this town who were using water-divining for the wrong reasons.'

'What did she mean by that?'

'She wouldn't tell me.'

'Well, it wasn't much good telling you anything.'

Helen's temper flared. 'It was a warning! Can't you see that?'

'What about?' He faced her for the first time.

'Oh never mind!'

They rode in silence until they reached the bridge. He stopped in the middle and they lifted their bicycles on to the path and leant on the balustrade, looking down into the river.

After a while he said, 'Tell me what she said.' He licked his lips. 'If you're going to speak to me any more.'

She could not answer. Her mouth was full of the need to cry. He saw it, and anguish made him thin and clumsy. 'Sorry,' he said.

Her tears nearly came. She fought them, and after a

moment she shuddered and was able to speak. 'She told me why she didn't let you have the twig.'

'She didn't like me,' he said.

'No. She does like you, but she's afraid for you. She doesn't want you to go spreading it about that you're a water-diviner, because she thinks you might get mixed up with the people she doesn't like.'

'Why me and not you?'

'I don't know.'

He gazed down into the water. After a while he said, 'Sometimes there's so much I don't understand I think I'm going crazy.'

'Let's take the book back,' she said.

'That's a good practical suggestion,' he said. He smiled.

'I've never seen anybody change as quickly as you do,' she said.

The long curve of houses by the river was a concave dish which captured the sun and focused it. They drifted along the brink like ash in a furnace.

'This is it,' said Dick.

They stopped in the centre of the curve where the stone front of the big house rose above them, tall and square and bright.

'I'll wait for you,' said Helen.

'No. Come on.'

High black railings guarded a gravel forecourt. The heavy gate shuddered stiffly as he pushed it open, and she followed him in. Three wide steps led up to the front door. They climbed them and she felt exposed. All she wanted to do was go home. Dick pressed the bell. No sound reached them from inside.

'It's like nudging an elephant,' he said. He put his thumb on the button again just as one half of the tall double door opened.

'Well, Mr Dodds! This is a surprise.'

Helen heard the voice, but Mrs Knowles was still out of sight, hidden by the other half of the door.

'Come in.' The voice was pleased. 'I've just been talking about you.'

'There's somebody with me,' said Dick.

'Oh.' A head appeared with the voice. Alarm in the eyes and then a sudden smile. 'A girl. For a moment I thought . . .' She paused. 'I thought you were alone.'

She stepped back for them to enter.

There was a small lobby and then, through glass doors, Helen could see the black and white tiles of the hall. It was circular, a ring with a black and white pattern. And the hall was as tall as the house; like a tower in the centre of the building. A staircase curved round the walls and it was not until it reached above the ground floor that there were any windows. At the bottom they walked in the dim green light where the heels of Mrs Knowles's shoes tapped and echoed like the drip of water in a well.

She opened a door in a dark alcove and led them into the big room Dick knew where the sun lay on the carpet. No noise penetrated from outside. They walked across to a large fireplace where a Japanese screen covered the cold grate and a marble mantelpiece jutted into the room like an elegant cliff face.

'And this is?' Mrs Knowles waited to be introduced.

'Helen Johnson,' said Dick. 'Mrs Knowles.'

They shook hands and sat down. The marble towered over them and Helen was nervous. But so, she noticed, was Mrs Knowles. A small woman, good looking and well dressed. She offered them cigarettes and when they refused she said, 'No, of course not,' but lit one herself. 'I shouldn't do this. People, doctors and people, keep telling me not to.' She puffed the smoke out quickly, laid the cigarette in an ashtray and forgot about it.

Dick said, 'We just met Mr Dawson.'

'Ah, Mr Dawson. Isn't that a coincidence?'

'Yes. And I had the book with me.' Dick held out the Shelley.

But she did not take it. Suddenly she was searching around the edges of her chair as though she had lost something. After a moment, Dick put the book on a little table by his side. He saw her glance sideways as though to make sure she no longer had to touch it, and then she raised her head.

'Where have you been with it?' The question was blunt, like an accusation.

'Down the river.'

Harshness in his voice. Helen, spectator, saw their eyes lock.

'It belonged to my husband.' She sat very straight. Haughty, offended.

Dick matched her. 'It's come to no harm.'

There was a pause. Helen watched the silent battle. And then Mrs Knowles said, and her face softened slightly as though she was trying to smile, 'And what would you say if I told you I knew where you had been and when?'

Helen saw Dick shrug. It seemed insolent. But suddenly the haughtiness crumbled and Mrs Knowles was searching for a second cigarette while the other still burned. As she fumbled, Helen saw the furniture in the room for the first time. Tables and chairs stood alone or in groups. Their thin legs touched the carpet daintily.

'No mystery,' said Mrs Knowles. 'Don't be alarmed. Somebody saw you and told me.'

'Who was that?' said Dick.

She ignored the question. 'It was last night. You were hurtling through the night like a thing possessed.'

'Where did this person see me?'

'Just somewhere down by the river.'

Her smile was secretive, exasperating. Dick took his eyes from her and turned to Helen. His face had no expression, no chink in his armour for Mrs Knowles to penetrate. And Helen dared to ask a question.

'Was this person there the night before that?' The staggering, falling creature in the track.

Two cigarettes burned together in the ashtray. 'Were you?' It was said with an edge of malice.

Helen did not reply. The silence tautened and sang like strings at breaking point. Slowly Mrs Knowles lowered her head and stirred fallen ash with a burnt matchstick. Her ankles were crossed under her chair, her forearms rested on the arms of the chair and, after a moment, her hands hung limply. She was responsible for the lull. She let it linger before she raised her head.

'You two say nothing,' she said.

Her face was smooth; she looked younger.

They did not reply.

'But you know much,' she said.

Still they sat and said nothing. In the big room, silence gathered like a monument.

'Mr Dodds,' Mrs Knowles spoke softly. 'I let you into a secret not long ago. I told you about the dark side of my house, and the other. Why have you become involved?'

Perhaps it was not too late to get free. 'I'm not,' he said.

'You are.' Her face was calm. Her words were sure. She waited for a reply but he said nothing. 'No?' she said. 'Then let me tell you what has happened to me.'

Two people walking. She began there. Far out in the fen. A hot, marvellous day.

'Then I saw this object.'

Black, blunt finger. It beckoned across the mud.

'Do you remember?' she said. 'I told you about it the other evening.'

Not quite, not quite. All she had told him was about how the river affected her. Not the stump in the mud. But he had seen the hole where it had been. Coldness crept over their skin.

'I think it was the body,' she said. 'The one they talk about.'

'What body?' Dick's voice was small.

'The one they say guards King John's Treasure.'

A shutter blinked in his eye. He saw her plain. A rich neurotic. From far away he came back to here and now, and he groaned.

'Mr Dodds?' She was plaintive, not understanding his new attitude. He looked into a face turned childlike, a believer in the story that King John had lost his Crown Jewels in the marsh all those centuries ago.

He spoke gently. 'What body? I know about the treasure, but I don't know about the body.'

'He was one of the guards,' said Mrs Knowles. 'When the jewels sank into the mud he stayed with them. They say he will kill anyone who gets too close.'

78

He was older than she, older in his mind. He laughed. 'Well, you haven't got anything to worry about,' he said. 'The Crown Jewels, if there ever were any, were lost near the town. Not anywhere near the coast.'

He spoke scornfully to jar her out of her fear. But she smiled, wanly, as though she knew more than he did, and anger rose in him to crush this superiority out of her.

'The log's gone!' he said.

Her fragile smile did not alter. 'Yes,' she said, 'but how did you know?'

It was as though, showing off, he had run over the edge of a cliff. His anger streamed away from him. Defence-less, he told her about the river dare, the boat, and the mud. She was there with him while Helen watched.

'And there was a trail leading from that place,' he said. 'A trail in the air.'

The woman's fear grew. 'Trail?' she said.

Dick nodded. He and Mrs Knowles were linked. Helen saw them drifting away from her. 'No!' Her voice cut down between them. 'It's something else. We found out this afternoon.'

This afternoon. Mrs Shepherd. The little house. It seemed long ago.

'Water-divining,' said Helen. 'We found out it was water-divining.'

Dick looked at her, blankly, still lost at the river mouth, but as his head turned the woman shuddered, coming free of the dream. 'Water-divining?' she said.

And Helen put facts before her, facts as hard as the twig that had bitten her fingers. It was like leading someone on stepping stones across a river, and the woman clung to her words until she was safe. Then suddenly she relaxed.

'Water-diviners,' she said. 'I always knew there was some strange power in you, Mr Dodds.'

Dick shrugged. 'Helen as well,' he said.

'Yes, of course,' said Mrs Knowles. She paused, and then said. 'I think I must apologize to both of you. I really am very much to blame for frightening you.'

'You didn't.' Dick did not want her to dominate him again.

'Oh yes I did,' she said. 'I led you into all this. First of all I tell you how the river affects me so that you risk your life exploring it at night. And then all this business about the log. I am to blame, really I am.'

Dick shrugged again.

'Tom will be annoyed with me for involving you like this.'

'Tom?' he said.

'Mr Miller. The man who was with me at the river mouth. Do you know him?'

Dick shook his head.

'I don't really think I should tell him about this, he will be annoyed.' She gave a little, lady-like laugh. 'He gets so cross when my imagination carries me away.'

There were questions to be asked but she gave them no chance. She was in charge again. Standing up, she said, 'Thank you so much for returning the book. And it really has been pleasant meeting you, Miss Johnson.'

She was quite composed and her movements were definite. She smoothly directed them from the room and within moments they were out in the sun, and the door, after polite good-byes, closed behind them. If there was a mystery, they were excluded.

15

They stood on the top step in the sun.

'Well,' said Dick, 'what was all that about?'

'Let's get away from here.' Helen led the way to the gate and was pulling at it before Dick reached her. They went through. 'Now shut it,' she said. Iron thudded against iron and jammed tight. 'That's where she belongs,' said Helen. 'Behind bars.'

She was cycling towards the bridge before Dick caught up with her.

'What's up?' he said.

'She's mad, that's what.' Helen's head was down, glowering at the road.

'But some funny things have happened,' he said. 'You can't explain them all away.'

'Yes I can. All of them.'

'Well who was it saw me riding through the fields the night I saw you?'

'That friend of hers, of course. Her precious Tom Miller.'

It was beginning to seem ridiculous. Dick wanted to laugh. 'But what about that hole in the mud where the log had been?'

'Who knows it was the same place? She's just making the whole ridiculous thing up.'

They crossed the bridge.

'What are we going to do, then?' said Dick. Her passion had taken charge.

'I'm going home,' she said. 'I've had enough of it!'

He rode with her without speaking. The town fell behind. They could breathe again.

'It's strange, though,' he said, 'How people's feelings seem to cross and get tangled. That's what's been happening, isn't it?'

'I suppose so.'

'You and me.' His mouth was dry. He dared himself to speak. 'That's still all right, isn't it?'

She nodded.

They rode a little further and then, still without looking at him, she said, 'I can't come out tonight, I've got to stay in.'

She gave no reason.

'Tomorrow?' he said.

'If you like.' She did not mean to be cruel, but she knew the words hurt.

'All right,' he said. 'Sometime tomorrow.'

He slowed, but she could not make herself pleasant to him and gradually she edged ahead.

'Good-bye,' he said.

'Good-bye.' She only half-turned towards him because of the tears in her eyes. She heard him stop but did not look round. At her back the distance between them grew.

She blinked, and the tears came at last, gently putting their marks down her cheeks.

He stood and watched until she was out of sight.

16

She rode away, dwindling into the narrowing road, flickered through the long grass at the corner and was gone.

Alone. Every single connection cut. The wide earth stretched out and out and floated like a leaf under the sky. Free of them all, he wanted to sing.

He could call them to him if he wished, Helen most easily of all. Mrs Knowles he was master of; Jim would be with him if he asked; and Mrs Shepherd knew the power of his gift.

He breathed the air deeply. In the brightness of the sunshine and the flatness of the land he stood alone. He dropped the bicycle on the verge and turned in the road with his arms outstretched. 'I am the key in the lock of the world,' he said. He let himself believe it for a moment. Then he picked up his bike. 'And I'm also mad.' But he was happy. The pressures were off. Tomorrow he would see Helen again. He laughed and rode.

'But I want to know more,' he said aloud. 'I want to know who wanders in the night like me. And why.' He fell silent, thinking. Only one person could tell him more. He spoke aloud again. 'Very well, I shall go to the sorceress at the core of the mystery. Mrs Shepherd, you shall guide my next step.'

He rode among the little houses like a man coming in from the desert, eyes narrowed by scorching winds. The kids who rolled in the gutters parted to let him through, and in the coolness of the passage between the houses the gate opened when he pushed.

Mrs Shepherd was having her tea in the room with the dark furniture and the blue flicker of her telly. She let him in without a word and without a smile. She fetched a cup and poured him tea. They sat and watched a face on the screen saying words and letting itself be erased when there were pictures to illustrate the words, and when the news was delivered she switched it off.

'You came back then,' she said, her back to him.

He sat back in his chair, the dark wood of the arms curling to each side of him.

'Yes,' he said.

'Where's that sweet little girl?'

'Gone home.'

Mrs Shepherd's eyes were on him. 'Quarrel?' she said.

'A bit,' he said.

'With you, my lad, that's no wonder.'

'But I . . .' He did not intend to finish the sentence.

She smiled then, knowing what he felt. 'She's got you.'

Dick nodded. It was what he wanted to be told.

'You've got a bit of nerve to come wandering into my place like this, haven't you?' she said.

'Well,' he said, 'I don't know why I did it.'

'But you're so shy,' she said. She was mocking.

'I suppose so.'

'And conceited as old Nick himself.' But she was smiling. 'You made that little girl tell you what I told her, isn't that so? And now you think you've got a right to know more.'

Dick leant forward and looked into a teacup that stood

84

on the tray in front of him. 'I want to know who the people are you warned us against.'

'Of course you do,' she said. 'Because you can't bear to be left out of anything.'

'Are you going to tell me?'

'Why should I?'

'So I shall know my enemy.'

'Now there's a thing,' she said. 'Why should anybody be an enemy of yours?'

'I'll tell you what's been happening,' said Dick. He glanced at her. Her round face was kindly. She knew she had made him climb down, and she was not going to make it difficult for him.

The mud, he got no further than the mud on the night of his river trip.

'Boy!' Her voice rang out, as though to stop him telling her any more.

'It's all right,' said Dick. 'I got away. It doesn't frighten me any more. Not much.'

He was going on to tell her about Helen and Mrs Knowles, but now she wanted to speak. In the dim room her plump face was pallid, ill.

'I told you, boy, you had the gift. It's as great as mine. The same. Now I've got to tell you more, so just you listen to me. It's more than hidden water with us. We pick up more than that. There's old and hidden things in the world and we know about them. Oh I wish to God we didn't!'

In the back room of a little house in a hidden street, two people who had picked up a secret they did not want.

'I've kept out of it,' she said. 'All my life I dreaded it. I walk along a street and I shudder. Some places I know of where I can't go because of what's happened there. I've asked, believe me I have, but nobody knows, and I don't either, but a horrible feeling comes like the end of the world, and you know what I mean.'

'Yes,' said Dick. At the back of his neck a feeling as though a hand was gripping him.

'I've been down the river, too,' she said. 'Same place as you. Not long ago either. Don't go there no more.'

'Why?' said Dick.

Mrs Shepherd sighed. 'You won't be satisfied till I tell you. Now listen you here, Dick Dodds, I remember your name and if you so much as breathe a word of this to a living soul I shall . . .'

She broke off and he looked into the glint of her glasses. 'I promise,' he said.

'There's such a thing as King John's Treasure, isn't there?' she said. 'Or supposed to be.'

'Supposed to be,' he said.

'Well you'd know more about it than me. All I know was that he buried it somewhere hereabouts all those years ago.'

'No,' said Dick. 'He lost it in the fens when his wagons sank in the mud.'

'Same thing. They've been looking for it ever since, haven't they? I've read bits in the paper.'

'Yes,' said Dick. 'But I don't reckon they'll ever find it because I don't think he ever did lose his Crown Jewels.'

'Boy, you are right. Stands to reason he never did anything so stupid, but there's folks who'll believe anything, and I've come across a few.'

'Because you're a dowser?'

'You've hit it. They think that if I was to walk over them old jewels I'd know.'

He smiled, but she said, 'It isn't so crazy as it sounds, because I can pick up metal and that; it's not just water. I been out with plenty of them in my time, and you should have seen the old junk they've dug up. And their faces – you've never seen such greedy old fools.'

She was laughing and Dick laughed with her. She was poor and still she despised treasure hunting.

'Well now, I was out only a few weeks back with one gentleman doing the same thing. He was quite nice, better than them really greedy ones. Said he was doing it just to get the history books right, and he said that if we found anything he was going to give it to the nation. Well you can believe that or not, just as you like, but I said I'd help. Usual fee, of course. Sometimes I say good old King John, I'm the only one who's made a bit out of that damned old treasure he never had or never lost.'

She was proud.

'Well I went out in his car. A bit secret, you know. He wouldn't pick me up here, I had to go out and around a bit to where I was to meet him. I thought he was going to the usual place where they all go, just a little bit down the river, but he kept on driving. On and on he went and I thought, well, Alice Shepherd, you've got a right one here, he's going to take you all the way to King Solomon's Mines. But I didn't mind. I didn't pay much attention to where we was going until damn me if he didn't stop the car right down the river as far as you can go. You know where that old lighthouse is, where the road ends?'

The amusement had gone out of her voice.

'You know where we are, boy, don't you?'

No need to answer. He waited.

'We got out then and started to walk. There's a path, if

87

you remember, right out to the end of the river and the
marshes. It was a grey old day, I remember, and pretty
damned cold and I don't walk all that well, but he kept on
a-going. On and on and the breeze coming in off the sea.
I would have turned back. I would have, even though he
said he'd double what he was going to give me, but he
kept saying how important it was to him, and so on I
goes. And when he was out there all alone on a bit of bank
he tells me to get out my dowsing rod and begin to try.
Well I did, of course, even though I knew it wasn't a bit
of good. We walked and we walked and he was getting
more and more excited, tense like, but my switch was as
quiet as a lamb. Never a twitch. And then, all of a sudden, I stopped. "I don't go no further," I said. "Why not?"
he says. "Because it ain't no good," I said. "There's
nothing here." And there wasn't, but that isn't why I
stopped.'

A grey sky over the marshes. The cold wind off the
mud.

'I was frit,' she said. 'That was a bad, bad place. Something real horrible. All around me. You know it, boy;
don't you? You felt it in the night. And you was alone.'

Dick was thin and cold inside his clothes.

'How you got through that,' said the little woman, 'I
shall never know.'

'No,' said Dick.

She was looking at him shrewdly. 'It gave you a big
fright, I can see that. But it's over now. You can forget
about it.'

'Can I?' he said. He thought of the stump, the trail,
Mrs Knowles.

'Of course you can. Whatever it was happened down

88

there was long ago, finished with. Just stay away, that's my advice to you.'

She paused. He waited, but she was saying no more.

'It's the body, I suppose.' He spoke quietly, disguising his annoyance, just letting her know he was in the secret.

'What body!' An angry jab of words.

'With the Treasure,' he said.

'I don't know what you're talking about!'

She knew nothing, and terrifying thoughts were forming in her mind. She looked ill. Now it was he who had power over her and he did not want it. But he had to speak. He told her of the man lost in the mud, but he spoke gently, diminishing it for her. 'It's an old wives' tale,' he said.

'Maybe.' She was very frail.

'Besides,' he said, 'it can't be that because the Treasure was lost near here, not down there.'

'No,' she agreed, 'no.'

And he could not tell her of the trail. She was too old for such a fear. He waited. The edges of her nostrils were blue. Breathing was difficult for her. But she had something to say.

'You know, son,' she said. 'You and me.' She had to pause to breathe. 'Two of a kind. I can see myself in you when I was a girl. Things like that horrible place down the river used to worry the living daylights out of me. And I didn't go looking for them like you do.' She had to pause again and he began to speak but she held up her hand to stop him. 'Body, you say. I don't know nothing about that and I don't want to. All I know is that there's things that happened in the past that made a mark, and some of us detect them and some of us can't. But I'll tell you what

– it's my belief they can't affect you if you don't meddle with them. So take my advice and leave it alone and forget about it. I've never meddled and I never will, and that's final.'

'You're right, Mrs Shepherd,' he said. He would not involve her any deeper, but he knew it could not finish there for him. He had to find out one more thing. He tried to make it sound as though it didn't matter much to him. 'Who is the man trying to find King John's Treasure?'

Her mouth shut tight.

'Well it doesn't matter, I suppose,' he said. 'I shan't ever come across him.'

And that made her think. 'Now just you hang on a minute,' she said. Her old sharpness was coming back. 'Suppose it do get around that you've been seeing me. That Pat has got a mouth the size of I don't know what. He just might get to hear about you. Well I don't know; you being you might want to help him and I reckon you're best out of all this.'

A pause, then she made up her mind. 'Now I'm going to tell you, Master Dick Dodds, and I don't think I would if it wasn't for that little girl. I'll tell you so as you won't be caught off your guard. He lives in one of them houses up the Avenues, and his name's Miller, and all I have to say to you is keep away from him!'

17

It was getting late. Outside, the narrow street was full of stale heat. The red brick of the houses seemed to be powdering into dust, slowly burning in the sun's rays. He had left the old woman without saying more. He rode slowly. Miller and Mrs Knowles. Some game they were playing. A madness in their minds, frightening each other – and him. Minds could affect minds. Why was he involved? What right had they to pull him into their play-acting? Let them get on with it. Mrs Shepherd was right; it was best to leave them alone.

He was weary. He slouched as he rode. Tomorrow he would see Helen. She would clear his mind.

He left his bike in the yard at the back of the house and went into the kitchen. It was long after tea-time and the table was bare, but he heard voices in the front room. His father was home. A blessed relief. Formality, politeness; for once he needed them. And he heard the chink of tea-cups. They were having a late meal. He washed his hands. He combed his hair.

'We're just beginning. Sit down, my boy.'

His father was a rock in a business suit. A phrase for Mrs Knowles, and she could go to hell.

His mother was a twittering bird, happy that her rock sat so solidly beside her. 'You look tired, Dick,' she said.

'Exhausted,' he said.

'Nice cup of tea will do you the world of good.'

'Hot tea cools you off,' said his father. 'One of the stranger facts of life.'

'Yes,' said Dick. They sat at a small circular table as though they were in a restaurant. The small talk would circulate.

'We've had a visitor this afternoon.' His mother, pouring tea, pressed one finger delicately on the lid as she tilted the teapot.

Dick gave her the words her smile demanded. 'Oh yes?' he said.

'Your friend from the literature class. Mrs Knowles.'

Even here. The bread in his mouth was dry.

'She's a very pleasant woman,' said his father.

'Isn't she?' said his mother.

They had been honoured. Wealth had entered their door.

'What did she want?' said Dick.

His tone was incorrect. 'She thinks highly of you.' His father was gently encouraging him to be respectful.

'I wrote some things that old Rob Dawson liked,' said Dick. 'He read them out.'

'Yes,' said his mother, 'and you never said.'

'Oh yes he did,' said his father.

'Well that's me,' said his mother, 'in one ear and out the other. But they must have been good, Dick, because she wants to see them again.'

Any excuse. Mrs Knowles was determined to snare him.

'I would have got them for her,' said his mother, 'but I know I daren't touch your papers.'

'They're only rubbish,' said Dick.

'Nonsense.' His father was sitting back, both hands pressed on the table, beaming.

'Oh well, I'll take them to her one day,' said Dick. 'Is that all she wanted? She's a bit crazy.'

'Don't be like that,' said his mother.

'Artistic people are,' said his father. A worldly-wise twinkle.

Father, Father, you're a mile away from me. But Dick smiled back. 'You're right, Dad. They're nuts.'

A pause. His mother fidgeted, looking at her plate, preparing a little revelation.

'And she told us something else.' Coyly. Wait for it. 'She said you went to see her with a girl.'

And everybody, even his father, looked down at the table.

Dick spoke quickly. 'It was Helen Johnson, I knew her at school.' A lie.

'Ever such a nice girl,' said his mother. 'She was quite taken with her.' But now her tone was hurt. She should have been the first one to meet the girl.

'I'd only just met her,' said Dick. 'She just happened to be there. Honestly.' Traitor and liar.

But his father was laughing. A rich chuckle. 'Don't embarrass him, Mother.'

'Well he's never brought a girl home.' She seemed to ask for pain.

'Do you want him to?' His father was sly. It worked.

'Of course I do. You know I do.' But she had never suggested it.

'Well I will,' said Dick. Committed. A sort of delirious agony made him happy and hungry.

Later that night he sat alone on the park gate in the tall cave of trees. It was very quiet; only the night noises, the open mouth of the park held up to the stars to catch a whisper that seemed to come down from the sky.

His mind accepted everything. The great calmness of the world and all the business that was yet to be finished. The things he understood and those he didn't. Tomorrow he would meet Helen.

18

He slept well and late. Early in the afternoon he cycled out to meet her.

Shy? Why should he be? But his mouth was dry as he turned into her yard. The door was open and inside, somewhere through the squares of receding doorways, a dim movement.

'Hello,' he called. It might be her mother.

But Helen came to him from the depths of the house, alone. She was caught by surprise and suddenly felt frowsty – the old dress, the worn shoes – and he saw her unshielded.

'They're out,' she said. It was a defence.

Relief unstiffened him but still he was awkward. 'Sorry I'm so early,' he said.

'Look at me!' she said, apologizing. She stepped back into the house, but he stood waiting to be asked. 'Come in,' she said.

The kitchen was big, not like his at home.

'It's a mess,' she said. It embarrassed her. 'I'm supposed to be clearing up.'

'I'll help.'

They stood apart; arm's length. 'Unbridgeable distance,' he said.

'What do you mean?' Eyes that were wide and dark. Eyes.

He approached clumsily. An object in space. She let him. Eyes open. And still open when the warmth of her skin reached him and her lips touched his.

And then, after that, the need for words. 'In the night,' he said, 'I sat on the park gate.'

She put her hands on the side of his head and kissed him again.

'It wasn't pitiful,' he said. 'I didn't mind.'

'I know,' she said.

'A big distance doesn't matter,' he said.

'No,' she said. 'But it's nicer close.'

'Female!' he said.

'Very well.' She pushed him away.

He put out his hand until their fingertips touched and ached, and she blinked and shuddered and said, 'Now you're going to do the washing up while I get changed.'

'Female,' he said. 'Housewife.'

'And a damned good job I am,' she said.

She fended him off, wriggled away as he tried to hold her when she went to the sink, filled the bowl for him and put the dishcloth in his hand. 'A present for you.'

He bowed, and she left the room.

When she came back she said, 'Keep away from me. My mother and father will be in for coffee in a minute.'

'We've got to go,' he said.

'Are you frightened they'll guess what you've been up to?'

'No,' he said, and then before she could interrupt, 'I went to see Mrs Shepherd again yesterday.'

'Oh no!'

'Well I had to do something after you left me.'

'Don't bring that up again,' she said.

'I reckon that's finished with,' he said. They smiled. 'But there is something going on.'

'I don't want to get in any more of it, Dick, honest I don't. They're all a bit mad.'

'Well so are we. There's that trail, don't forget.'

'I know, I know. But there is some explanation. We were frightened then, weren't we? We made ourselves believe it.'

He told her then about Mrs Shepherd and the place on the bank where she felt evil coming up from the mud. 'I felt it too,' he said. 'That night I took the boat.'

Her eyes dropped and after a moment she said, 'You must have been pretty scared that night.'

'All right,' he said. 'I'll admit all that. But Mrs Shepherd told me why she went down there in the first place.'

He was telling her about Miller and King John's Treasure when her mother came in. She was wearing her working clothes. Dick was standing awkwardly, an interloper.

'Coffee's not ready, I see,' said Mrs Johnson. She wrinkled her eyes, looking from one to the other.

'Mother!' said Helen, warning her. 'He's just finished the washing up.'

'She's got you at it early,' said Mrs Johnson. She watched the beginning of his blush and then bustled her daughter about. 'Come on then, slow coach, get the kettle on.' But she couldn't resist turning to Dick and saying, 'You don't know what you're letting yourself in for.'

'If you go on like this when Dad comes in, I'll never speak to you again,' said Helen.

Mrs Johnson looked at Dick, pursed her lips for a moment and then began to laugh.

But when Mr Johnson came in the mischief had gone. He was a silent, shy man and they talked politenesses until they were able to leave.

Clouds were in the sky for the first time, high and feathery, the bright fading scars of a distant storm.

'Where are we going?' said Helen.

'Mrs Knowles wants to see me,' said Dick, 'but I ain't going there.'

'I wouldn't go with you even if you did.'

'You don't like her, do you?' said Dick.

'Not much.'

'She's all right,' he said. 'But I'll tell you what. We ought to go and see this man Miller.'

Helen would not look at him. After a while she said, 'You promised.'

'Promised what?'

'You promised Mrs Shepherd you wouldn't go to see him.'

'Oh blast!' He had forgotten.

So there was nothing to be done.

'And I thought we were going to tie it all up,' he said. 'A clue from one, a clue from the other and we'd be out of it and free.'

Helen saw what he was trying to do. He enjoyed the mystery and the danger and did not want to lose it. But she had to keep away from those people.

'I'm sorry,' she said.

'Doesn't matter.' But he was almost sulking.

She was letting him down. He believed it. She could see it in the way he lifted his head and looked into the distance.

'There's one thing,' she said. It had nothing now to do with Mrs Knowles, Miller or Mrs Shepherd. 'We could go and see if the trail's still there.' He was interested. She had to be cautious. 'I mean at the place where we left off following it,' she said.

'That!' he said. 'That's only playing about with waterdivining.' He wanted to go down to the river mouth.

'It'd be something,' she said. 'Come on, let's try.'

He was persuaded, and she saw it.

'You don't always have to do something risky,' she said. 'Not for me.'

The wispy clouds lay in the top of the sky, far apart from each other like frail boats. A mile beneath their keels, the deep air stirred.

'We shall need twigs,' Dick said. 'Proper equipment.'

'And I bet you haven't got a knife,' she said.

'Why is it you're always right?' he said.

But they found a tree, he broke off a low branch and from it they got two forked twigs. They peeled off the bark and the switches were slippery and naked white.

'I can't even remember where we lost the trail yesterday,' he said.

'Oh yes you can.'

They circled until they came to the lane behind her father's orchard.

'Somewhere along here,' she said.

'I remember now,' he admitted.

They cycled slowly, the forked twigs wedged into their handlebars, not yet ready for use. The trail, when they crossed it, was faint, but both felt it. Not the horror of before, just a familiar shiver. They laid their bikes in the long grass of the verge.

'Now remember your lesson,' said Dick. 'Don't grip the twig too hard.'

'You don't know anything about it,' she said. 'You've never done it.' And it was she who had to show him how to lace the wand in his fingers.

'Who goes first?' he said.

'I do.'

He watched her walk in the gravel and dust at the edge of the road, the twig pointing directly ahead. At the place they knew it would happen, the twig quivered, a quick little shudder, and dipped. She kept walking along the verge and the thing fluttered in her hand.

'I feel it along here,' she said, 'it's strong.'

'My go.'

She stepped aside. 'I feel a bit weak,' she said, 'even after that.'

Dick walked into the line she had been travelling. He expected the old grey coldness and the sudden misery. It didn't come. Instead, a jab of pain in his fingers where the rod twisted down and then up, wanting to bite, burn, peck at him to get free, fly off.

He cried out. Struggled with it. 'The damned thing!' he shouted. 'It's after me!'

And it was Helen who saved him.

She pulled at his sleeve, dragged him away from the verge. His arms jerked and the twig, like a bird's bone, cracked. He flung it away, dead and broken.

'Ah!' he said. He hated it. Dead and disgusting.

But there was sudden joy in Helen. He was much more

afraid than she. And there was more. If this sort of thing had happened in the night his imagination would have leapt to huge terrors. And more still. If something similar had happened to Mrs Knowles, the whole threat of the river, the evil creature in the mud, could have grown from the ability they had to detect underground streams. And she was one of them, inside the mystery, but a mystery they could control.

'You'd best leave it to me,' she said.

He filled his lungs and emptied them slowly.

'All right,' he said. He felt a weakling, and she saw it. She said, 'If I lose it you can put me right.'

He was being humoured, but it made sense. For more than a hundred yards he walked beside her along the verge and although the switch made little movement in her hands she did not ask for help. They were beyond her father's orchard between fields of wheat, when she stopped.

'Lost it?' he asked.

'No. I was thinking about our bikes.'

'Doesn't matter about them,' he said. 'We'll fetch them in a minute. There's nobody out here to pinch them.'

They passed the mouth of a green lane on their left. A few paces beyond it he stopped.

'What is it?' she said.

'You're going the wrong way.'

'No I'm not.' She knew the twig was telling no lies. The way lay directly ahead. But he doubted her. She could tell by his face. 'What's happened?' she said.

He stepped to the verge and stood in the line she had been following. 'Is there water here?' he asked. Without the twig he could not be sure. She nodded. He walked back a few paces, turned into the lane and stood still.

At that moment the afternoon changed. A small movement in the air set the wheat fields whispering, then died. His back was turned to her. She freed one limb of the twig and let her hands drop to her sides. They stood, painted into the landscape, motionless.

Then, against the background of the hedge, he moved, turning slowly; side view, three-quarter view, full face.

Now her turn to move. She went towards him, stepping stiffly, mechanically cutting the distance between them. At his side she felt the coldness. Not water-divining. The trail.

They were at a crossroads. At this spot the trail crossed the hidden stream. Two separate things.

They stepped back.

'I see,' he said softly.

'What do you mean?' Helen was quivering.

'I mean I don't see. It's not water-divining, is it?' His mind was churning, beginning to bring up hidden things. Helen was afraid. 'Something else,' he said. 'Something else.' Excitement was licking him. He began to move into the lane, thoughtlessly.

'No!' she said.

He came back to her. 'Come on,' he said. 'It's broad daylight. Just let's see where this goes.' He would not think. He had to act. He held her hand and she went with him.

The lane was narrow and choked with grass. The hedges on either side were high and uneven. The trail went down the centre but they kept to one side. There could be no deviation along here even if they wanted to.

'Like a jungle,' Dick said. He dipped his head under a branch that straggled over the path. The grass was sometimes waist-high and clouds of little white moths lifted away from them. Deeper and deeper. 'What do you think this was?' he said. 'An old pathway across the fens?'

Helen looked back. A slight bend cut off the opening they had entered, and the far end was not yet in sight.

'I don't like it,' she said. Her voice was deadened by the leaves.

His face was tense, feeling again the force of the trail. She gripped his hand tightly. Grasses brushed their arms; in places, tall weeds grew head-height. She looked where she trod, her feet pressing into the dark tunnels of the undergrowth, and she wanted to go back. But he would not turn; not yet.

Ahead and to the right there was a ragged gap. 'Might be a way through,' he said.

The tall weeds stank.

'No further than that,' she said.

'It's a gate,' he said.

'When we get there I'm going no further.'

He walked quicker. Blue sky in the gap. They would be in the open again.

It was a gate to nowhere, grassed in. They could see that before they got there. The wooden bars were grey.

'Let's go back,' she said. 'There's nothing.'

He stopped. The smell of the mud. It was in his nostrils again. But there was the gate. Only a gate. He would reach it and go. Only a small dare.

He went forward with her. The last few paces. An arm's length from him.

And then, where the hedge clutched the gate-post, half-obscuring it, a round head was leaning from the leaves looking at them.

Dick heard Helen's whimper. Heard it. Heard it as the bars and bolts of his bones shot home.

Her sob again. And then the flood of his own blood washing fear away. The head was an old post. He saw it. A black, smooth, round, bald-headed old post.

He put his hand to the gate.

'Damn you!' He let the yell of his lungs hit the black head. Black. Wet. It shone in the sun. And he knew what he should have known before. It had come from the mud.

Behind, wild, Helen pulled.

The bald black head, faceless, moved.

His hand lifted from the gate. A claw.

The head slid; sighed into the deep grass and vanished.

A pigeon, bang, bang in the blue, clapped its idiot wings, and they smashed down the green grass as they ran.

His arm was round her once to lift her. Once. And out in the road he held her again when she stumbled.

Their bikes lay where they had left them, untouched.

18

All true. They rode shakily between the fields until the green lane was lost.

'I want to go home,' said Helen, 'and tell my mother.'

'Yes,' said Dick, 'I know.'

Into the main road where the cars went to and fro.

'She'd laugh at you,' said Dick. 'And me. She'd say it was me.'

'But we'd take her and show her, if my father would come.'

'A log,' said Dick. 'A black old log. It's nothing more than that.'

'You don't believe it, then?' She faced him, almost angry, made a fool of.

'Some things fit together. But we need to know more.'

She saw he was pale, as frightened as she was, but he would never admit it.

'Oh, Dick, can't we just leave it?'

He did not answer immediately. But then he said, 'Will it leave us?'

Worse than the green lane. Worse than that black smooth head. But it was the truth, and she started to cry. They stopped and he stood beside her as the cars went by. Her head was bowed, ashamed for him to see her face, and he waited, shielding her from the faces in the cars. At length, from her sleeve, she took a handkerchief, and dried her face.

'Sorry.' She blew her nose. Sniffed. She looked up. 'I know I look terrible,' she said.

'Beautiful,' he said. He kissed her. The salt of tears.

'Somebody will see,' she said.

'To hell with them.'

A car came and he raised his hand to wave at it but she held his wrist.

'I'll do whatever you say,' she said.

'There's only one person to see.'

She nodded.

'We might as well get it over with,' he said.

They were glad of the busy road and then the town that shut out the countryside. Helen was troubled about how she looked, but it was only her eyes that showed she had been crying and that very little. She forgot about it as they rode up to the big house.

The front door was a deep and glossy green. Dick's hand rested on it as he pressed the bell. It burned like hot metal.

They waited. Dick pressed the bell again. 'What if she's not in?' he said.

'But she wanted to see you. Your mother said so.' Helen was anxious to see her now. She stood back and looked at the windows. All were empty. In a big house like this it must be possible to get beyond the sound of the bell.

Dick said, 'Let's go round the back.'

Across the road the river ran low. They tried not to look at it as they rode to the corner that would take them behind the house. They were in the shade there, under the long wall which hid the gardens, and once again Dick found it difficult to pick out Mrs Knowles's gate. They tried two. Both were locked.

'Blast!' Dick was angry. He pushed his fist against a pair of garage doors that stood in the wall. They swayed slightly. 'Let's try this,' he said. He lifted the latch and the door opened.

He looked inside. 'It's her car,' he said. 'Let's see if we can get in this way.'

He leant his bike against the wall but Helen hung back. 'We'd better not,' she said. It was like breaking in.

'Well if her car's here I reckon she's not out,' he said.

Timidly, Helen followed. Dick shut the door behind them. It was cool inside, and dim. They edged round the car to where a single window looked into the garden. A trailing plant hung across the window, but they could see rose bushes, a sundial, a patch of lawn. The house itself was out of sight. There was a door by the window. Dick turned the handle and it opened, letting a streak of sunlight cut across the cold garage floor.

We mustn't. The words were in Helen's head, but she said nothing.

'Come on.' Dick walked out boldly, surprising himself. 'She knows we're not burglars.' He closed the door noisily.

The garden was completely enclosed, partly paved. Flowers trailed from a stone trough beside a path. It was a private place, and they hesitated before they went forward. The garden was larger than they imagined and they were deep among its paths before they caught their first glimpse of the house. Through the trees they saw the red brick of its back wall, its big windows evenly spaced, climbing one above the other until the overhanging branches of the trees cut them off.

A long, narrow lawn led up to the house. They paused at the edge, still under the shade of the trees. Bees hummed in the garden undisturbed. There was no movement at any of the windows they had in view. They stepped out on to the grass, innocent callers, ready to smile and speak.

As they came out from under the leaves they saw the top storey. The highest windows, like the others, were vacant. They concentrated on the ground floor. Dick picked out the tall window through which the sun would be streaming on to the carpet in the big room.

The grass made their footsteps very quiet, stealthy in spite of themselves. Out in the centre of the lawn, concentrating on the big window.

Helen tugged at Dick's arm. He jumped and his head jerked round.

'What?' he said.

She was looking up, beyond him. Her mouth was open

He lifted his head.

The flat red wall of the house rose to a heavy stone parapet that cut squarely across the sky. A straight line. Except in the centre. Mrs Knowles, her smooth arms folded on the stone, was looking out and away across distant fens they could not see.

She was motionless. A profile against the blue. She seemed to be posing. She was good-looking enough. And Helen was jealous.

Dick called her name, but she did not hear.

'Louder,' said Helen.

'Mrs Knowles!'

The profile turned, elegantly, and she looked down. She was not surprised. She smiled. Even from below they saw the blueness of her eyes.

'The door is open,' she said. She did not move.

'Might as well go in then,' said Helen. It was she who led the way to a paved verandah at the end of the lawn. Set between two windows was a door that was mostly glass. It led into a room they had not seen before. It had many bookcases, a large desk with a leather top. Dick paused in the middle and looked around. 'I like this,' he said.

'It's never used,' said Helen.

She was right. Everything was too still, too neat. It must have been Mr Knowles's room, when he was alive.

'Where now?' she said.

In a corner alcove, almost hidden, there was a door. It was Dick now who went first. The alcove was dim, and as he opened the door the coolness of the depths of the house came over them in a gentle cascade. Helen felt it on her arms. They went through into what at first seemed to be a deeper alcove, but then they saw the black and white floor of the circular hall and realized they had come out beneath the stairs.

A museum silence. They came out on to the circle of tiles. The light was faintly greenish, and from where they stood, at the base of the huge drum, the stairs spiralled up the wall from landing to landing until, at the top, they joined a circular balcony beneath a white dome.

'Shall we go up?' Helen's voice was too quiet to find the echo.

Dick nodded. They moved across to the foot of the stairs and began to climb. At each curved landing there was a window. The first, less than tree height, looked out over the garden. They climbed higher, circling the drum until the next window showed them the town. They went higher, turning away from the roof-tops until, from the back of the house, they saw over the trees into the road at the back. One more curving flight led to the balcony.

They looked down as they climbed, gripped the banisters tighter. Below them, shafts of sunlight made slanting bridges from wall to wall.

They came on to the balcony at the front of the house and looked out. Far below the river crawled thin and brown, cutting off the town, and losing itself between green banks like a snake sliding into the grass. They turned away. Above them the fluted ridges of the dome curved higher still, unreachable, and the balcony seemed frail. They were edging round it slowly when, directly opposite them, across the space, a door opened and Mrs Knowles stepped through.

They stood on opposite sides of a circle. They need never meet. That was Helen's first thought.

'I'm glad you came.' Mrs Knowles spoke quietly, but her voice reached them as though they stood side by side. She wore a thin summer dress of a darker blue than Helen's. She looked small; an ornamental figure near the high ceiling.

There was a moment's hesitation. Which way did they walk to meet? And then Mrs Knowles smiled and pointed, and they moved towards the only other window on the balcony, the one at the back of the house.

Mrs Knowles stood with one hand cupped in the other. Dick, tallest of the three, stood opposite, and Helen faced the centre of the window.

'We saw you from below.' Dick, awkward, waited for his intelligence to give him something better to say.

'It's hot on the roof.' But Mrs Knowles looked cool.

A moment's pause and then Helen and Mrs Knowles began to speak together. Then they both stopped.

'I'm sorry.' Mrs Knowles put a question in her voice.

'No,' said Helen. 'It doesn't matter.'

Mrs Knowles said, 'It does matter. I know you well enough, Helen.' It was the first time she had used her name. A barrier down. 'But really I ought to tell you why I wanted to see you. I want to take you to meet a man and tell him what you know.'

'Yes,' said Dick. Helen waited for him to tell about the black log, but he said nothing.

Then Mrs Knowles laughed. 'You know where we are, don't you?' She gestured with her hand, indicating the ring of the balcony. 'This is my magic circle. Over there,' she pointed across to the window at the front of the house, 'is the dark side. Here, we are on the light side. And it certainly is true; at the moment, anyway. Look.'

She pointed out of the window. They were above the nearest trees. Beyond the road the landscape was squared into fields and there was a thin scatter of buildings, but further out the flatness of the fens shimmered in the heat.

'Sometimes,' she said, 'I see something out there that is almost magical.

'Almost?' said Dick.

'Almost.' She spoke firmly. She pointed again. 'Somewhere about there I see a patch of bright silver. So bright it is hard to look at. Day or night it comes. I look for it because it helps me when the river threatens.'

Her Silver Fields, but she had avoided the name as though it was too fanciful. She was being practical. Something was slipping away. Now was the time to tell her. Dick opened his mouth. But Mrs Knowles sighed.

'I think it's all nonsense,' she said. She looked at them both. 'That's what I really wanted to tell you. Ever since you told me about water-divining I've been feeling happier. There seemed to be something pressing but now it's gone. I never used to get those fears when my husband was alive. Never. This was a lovely house then, although I never did like the river. Tom says it's all because I'm living here alone. Imagining things.'

There was some nervousness in her, as though she was afraid the memory would bring tears.

'But it's all going to alter soon.' Suddenly she put a hand on Helen's arm. 'Helen,' she said, 'this young man made it worse for me. He seemed to see everything I spoke about. He seemed to see it with his eyes. Really what I did was inexcusable. I involved him in a nightmare. My nightmare. But now you've pulled me out of it and I want you to come and meet Tom. Tom is sane. He puts your mind at rest.'

And Helen saw what was in Mrs Knowles's mind. She saw what Tom meant to her. Dick watched them smile at each other.

20

Down the staircase, talking. Dick behind the other two. They went out of the house a different way without going through Mr Knowles's study. Dick opened the garage doors and got into the back seat of the car beside Helen. They drove into the sunshine and, as they crossed the bridge, he held Helen's hand. The leather of the car seat was cool on their legs and backs.

'I'm a silly thing,' said Mrs Knowles. Behind her they were careful of their smiles in case she saw them in the mirror, but she was leaning forward concentrating on the traffic. 'I don't even know if he's at home this afternoon. He might be in his office. Why didn't I ring up?'

'Mr Miller?' said Dick.

'Yes. Do you know him? He's the solicitor.'

The solicitor. He might have known it would be somebody like that. 'No,' he said. Helen's hand squeezed his. A warning. 'No I don't know him.' His tone was pleasanter.

'You'll like him.'

They were almost through the town, but she stopped at a junction, waiting to turn across the traffic into a broad

road, tree-lined, the Avenues, where all the houses stood back, sealed off and protected.

'He was very good to me when my husband died.' Leaning forward again, waiting for a gap in the traffic. 'There was a lot of work to be done. I don't know how I would have ...' The gap came and she swung the car into a part of the town that was as cut off as Mrs Shepherd's streets. They turned into a driveway and shrubs fingered the sides of the car before letting them through into a gravelled space in front of the house. As they got out, the front door opened.

'Tom, I'm so glad you're in!'

As Mrs Knowles crossed the gravel towards him, Mr Miller stepped out of the porch. He was a tall man, and she went up very close to him, holding both his hands, so that he had to bend his head to look down at her. For a moment Dick thought they were going to kiss, but that was not Miller's style. He had a long face with a golf-course tan, and deep creases ran from the sides of his nose to the corners of his mouth. His smile faded to watchfulness as he raised his head to look at them.

'I've brought somebody to see you,' said Mrs Knowles. She introduced them.

Miller had a lean, hard hand. 'How do you do?' An easy voice, well controlled.

'They've had something to do with that business I was telling you about.'

'Oh?' His small dark eyes, made to seem smaller by his heavy eyebrows, darted from her to them and back again.

'No need to worry, Tom. I think we all understand each other now.'

'Well that's something to be hoped for.' He was gently

mocking her and, through her, them. 'Let's go in, shall we?' He half-turned to let them go in ahead of him. His hair, going grey, just came over the collar of his light-weight summer suit.

The hall was not large; a coat-stand and a telephone table at the foot of the stairs. Mrs Knowles led them straight through into a room at the side of the house. French windows looked out over a conventional garden, a lawn and neat borders puffed up with flowers like a calendar picture.

'Please be seated,' said Miller. He was affable. 'Something to drink? Tea or something?'

It was the sort of room Dick expected of the Avenues. Enough space for plenty of deep armchairs, a bureau in one corner, paintings in gilt frames. The sort of room his mother would love in the sort of house she wanted; a garden from a calendar, a room for afternoon tea.

'No tea for me, Tom. I know how long it takes you to make it.' Mrs Knowles was dealing with a bachelor. Helen and Dick said no thank you.

'Tom, you know how I've been feeling about the river recently; the terrible feelings I have about it.'

He nodded curtly. He did not care for this kind of talk.

'Well,' she went on, 'I was not alone in feeling them. Dick, here, has had the most extraordinary experiences; and Helen, too.'

By using their first names she was forcing an intimacy on Miller that he was not ready to accept. He sat squarely, his long hands folded under his chin. It was impossible to tell if his lawyer's face was interested or merely polite. She told him about the boat trip, and his little dark eyes flickered to Dick and away. Then the trail and what Helen had seen. She spoke excitedly, even gaily, but Miller interrupted.

'We all know what we're talking about, I suppose,' he said.

'Of course, Tom! That log in the mud that day we were out seeking King John's Treasure.'

Miller's anger was contained. His knuckles whitened and his heavy eyebrows came forward just a fraction. Nothing else. But he cut Mrs Knowles like a knife.

'I'm sorry, Tom.' She was pale. 'All I meant to mention was the log.'

'Has this young man been frightening you?'

'No, Tom, no!'

The eyes, hard and straight, swung to Dick. 'Did you remove that object from where we saw it? I know that it has gone.'

Battle. Dick's anger flashed as sharp as the eyes that tried to pierce him. Helen saw it. 'No!' she cried.

The crisis, all of it, swung to her. Three heads faced her. 'It wasn't us,' she said.

In a strange room, a frightened girl. Mrs Knowles said, 'Of course it wasn't! Tom, how could you?'

Like lightning conductors the women had picked the anger from the air and sent it to earth. The men were shamed.

Dick's breath was heavy in his throat and he could not speak. It was Miller who said, 'I think I owe you an apology.' His eyes did not rest on Dick for more than a moment.

Dick said, looking at Mrs Knowles, 'It was the same as you. We thought something happened.' He mumbled. The form of words for accepting an apology would not come.

'But, Tom,' said Mrs Knowles, 'I'm so relieved. It's all

been water-divining. All those terrible feelings. These two are water-diviners!'

The trail was not water-divining. But they had helped to make her believe it was and she was grasping at it now, eager to make the explanation hold. They hesitated and lost the chance to speak.

Miller was leaning forward and Dick at last had to look at him. When he smiled the long creases in his face curved and deepened.

'I have had experience with dowsers,' he said.

Dick nodded. 'I know.'

A shift of suspicion in the eyes again, then back to friendliness. 'Our Mrs Shepherd?'

'Yes.'

'Of course.' The eyes held him. A court-room scene. 'She told you about me?'

The answer had to be yes or no. 'Yes.'

Miller sat back in his chair abruptly and flourished his brown thin hands towards Mrs Knowles. 'I thought you were giving something away, but it was our awkward little dowsing lady.'

It was his apology to her and she was happy. 'Oh, Tom, tell them everything!'

He stood up swiftly, an actor's movement. 'It is the best tactics,' he agreed. 'And moreover I have already a guarantee that this young man will repeat nothing.'

'Of course he won't.'

'There is the little matter of taking away a boat without the owner's consent.'

'Tom, you wouldn't!'

The creases of his smile deepened. 'I have a lawyer's mind.'

'If you were to do anything about that . . .'

But his hand was waving again, dismissing it. 'All I want to impress on them is that what I am about to divulge is a private matter.'

'What about Mrs Shepherd?' It was Dick, speaking behind the standing man.

'I can deal with her.' He did not turn round.

'Do nothing,' said Dick. An order. The back of the tall man stiffened. 'She did not tell me who you were. She only wanted to keep me out of trouble.' It was a lie.

Miller was slow to turn round. Helen saw his face before Dick. He was calculating. At length he faced Dick, looking down at him.

'Shrewd,' he said. He began to laugh. 'It seems we are in each other's power.' He was laughing at himself. Dick, warily, smiled back.

'Very well,' said Miller. 'It's between us. Understood.'

He went to the bureau in the corner and, taking a key chain from his pocket, unlocked a drawer. He took out a fat folder.

'My hobby,' he said. 'Historical research into the drainage of the fens.'

'Liar,' said Mrs Knowles.

He inclined his head. 'As the lady says. It began as that and ended as a treasure hunt.' His flippancy vanished and he stated his case briefly and quickly. 'You know,' he said, speaking to Helen and Dick, 'that the sea, or at least the marsh, centuries ago came right up to the town itself. Agreed?' They nodded. 'The land was drained, the sea receded.' He drew maps from his folder and handed them over. 'What I have proved is that it was not only the water that retreated but that the land, or part of it, the part most muddy and waterlogged, tended to drift with it. Nothing remarkable in that. But . . .' an actor's pause '. . . I can show you, pretty conclusively, that this land drift is still continuing.'

Comment was required. 'Can it?' said Dick. 'Dry land?'

'Ah,' said the lawyer, 'that is the essence. *Dry* land? No indeed. Go down but a foot or two and all of the land hereabouts is far from dry. In places very wet indeed. So full of water, in fact, that it is still *flowing*. Now look.'

He pulled photographs from the folder, pictures of fen fields. 'Now mark this.' He pointed to two posts planted in the earth, one near the camera, the other distant. 'They are in line, are they not?' They were. 'But in this, taken from the same spot less than a year later, what do we see?'

'The posts aren't quite in line,' said Helen.

'Excellent. And there are others.' More photographs came out.

'But surely farmers notice this,' said Dick.

'I dare say.' Miller was smiling. 'But who knows what farmers notice?'

Dick looked sideways at Helen. Miller could be describing her father. Colour had mounted in her cheeks but she said nothing, and what Miller said next calmed her.

'It happens,' he said, 'only in a few places and in comparatively narrow channels. Here is a plan of those I have discovered. There are gaps, as you will notice.'

Dick studied it intensely, an idea in his mind. Miller began to speak but Dick said, 'Just a minute, I think one of them is the trail we've been following.' And Helen saw that his mind was changing, accepting new evidence, prepared to believe in the water-divining theory that Mrs Knowles had clutched at.

'You are probably right,' said the man. 'There's a lot of water there and you're a diviner.' But he was keener to get on to his next point. 'Now consider,' he said. 'King John crossed the marsh just here, near the town. The tide caught him and he lost his baggage train. It sank, according to contemporary accounts, in mud and quicksand and was never seen again.'

'And at least one poor man, too,' said Mrs Knowles.

'True.' But to the lawyer this was beside the point. 'Now all attempts to find the jewels have been along the line of the old causeway which is well known, but what if they were caught in one of the places where the land has continued to drift seawards?'

The answer was obvious but he wanted to hear it spoken.

'It would have been moving ever since,' said Dick.

Miller said nothing. He unfolded a large-scale map and laid it on the floor at their feet. He crouched, pointing with a long finger at a dotted line with crosses at intervals against which were dates.

'This is supposition, you must realize that, but it is possible that the wagon train and the jewels have, by now, almost reached the coast.'

His head was level with theirs, closer than they had been before. He was looking quickly from one to the other, excited.

'So that's why you went to the coast,' said Dick.

'Of course.' Miller stood up. 'And, leaving nothing to chance, I took old Mrs Shepherd in the hope that her remarkable powers may have been able to direct us nearer the spot.' Triumph and an edge of sarcasm in his voice.

'I think it's marvellous,' said Helen.

'But all the time I kept thinking of that poor man who was drowned,' said Mrs Knowles. There was anxiety in her blue eyes.

Miller laughed. 'I think my only mistake,' he said, 'was telling you that really rather silly little story I dug up.'

'Tom, you are callous. You think a few beastly jewels are more important than a man.'

Miller had his enthusiasm under control. All he did was smile and begin collecting his papers. There it was. Maps and photographs. Facts.

'Tom, I am grateful to you,' said Mrs Knowles. 'You've brought us all down to earth again.'

It was his role as a lawyer to sort things out. He was pleased with himself. But Dick held himself clear of their raft of fact.

'Mrs Knowles,' he said. 'You told us the other day that somebody had seen me one night down by the river when I was following the trail.'

'Oh, that,' she said, laughing. 'That was nothing.' Miller was replacing his papers in the bureau, locking the drawer. 'I was full of fancies then, wasn't I, Tom?'

It was something about which Miller did not want to speak. He spent a long time locking the drawer.

'That log,' said Mrs Knowles. 'I thought it was the body of the man you told me about. It was uncanny, wasn't it, Tom, the way Mrs Shepherd thought she felt something evil?'

'Just a shade hysterical.' He lifted his heavy eyebrows, making fun of women's fancies.

'Well,' said Mrs Knowles, 'after you'd told me about the guardian of the Treasure I really thought that that was him warning us off. I even imagined he was coming in-land after us. Perhaps I'm a water-diviner too and picked up the trail.'

She had not answered the question.

'But how did you know about me?' said Dick. 'Who saw me?'

A pause. Mrs Knowles did not want to answer. She dropped her eyes.

'I did!' Miller's voice was harsh. He disliked this questioning boy. Mrs Knowles glanced up quickly at the standing man and then hung her head.

Miller had the look of a man caught out in a secret, something that others would consider discreditable but in which he felt no guilt. He thrust his hands in his jacket pockets, thumbs out. 'My researches took me down there. I saw you.'

Another point cleared up. It was very simple. Why then was Miller standing there, dominating, prepared to bully anyone who questioned him? Why had Mrs Knowles fallen so silent?

And then, from the start of the day, a thought reached over, flicking across like a lizard's tongue. The green lane; the black and bald-headed stump.

Clear this matter up as well. Out with it. Dick began to speak. 'We were out riding in the fens this morning,' he said.

Helen knew what was coming. Why couldn't he let it rest? Miller was not a man to be pressed. 'It was lovely out there,' she said. A hint to Dick, a call for help.

Mrs Knowles came to life. 'The fens, the fens!' she said, as though she had heard enough about them. She stood up. 'I'm going to make some tea.'

And then Helen saw an escape. 'Dick's mother is expecting us,' she said. It was successful. Mysteries and questions were shattered and abandoned; they talked politenesses and a few minutes later Mrs Knowles's car was brushing the leaves of the driveway on their way out into the town again.

21

Neither Helen nor Dick said much as they crossed the town. They left the talking to Mrs Knowles. She talked of Tom, she talked of the weather and the fens, and laughed at her own fears. Tom had taught her to do that. 'You won't mention King John's Treasure to anybody, will you?' she said.

No, they promised.

They were glad to leave her. As they cycled back over the bridge, a breeze was blowing down the river. Helen felt it on her arms and legs and face; it lifted the pressure of the sun from her. And Dick was laughing.

'I don't see what there is to laugh about,' she said.

'Neither do I,' he said. 'I'm just glad to have escaped.' And then he added: 'Temporarily.'

She knew what he meant. 'We didn't tell them about that thing we saw this afternoon,' she said.

'Well, it was you who stopped me,' he said.

'I know.'

Traffic crowded them and Dick had to let Helen ride in front. She went with the cars, inching along, until in the market place Dick was able to draw alongside. They could see the Institute clock.

'Look at the time!' she said. 'I'll have to go.' But they both remembered the excuse she had given to get away.

'Come and have tea with us,' said Dick.

Neither of them wanted to do it. It was one more strain, but it had to be endured.

Dick's shame began at the backyard gate. With two bicycles in it the yard was crowded. At her house there was space. His mouth was dry as he opened the kitchen door. There was nobody there. He took her through quickly into the front room, leading the way. Both his parents were seated at the table.

Helen, burrowing into one more corner of the town, heard her heart-beat whisper in her ears. His father, the first to see her, rose with majestic politeness, putting his napkin beside his plate. Town, not country. A suit, not a farmer's shirt-sleeves.

Dick was mumbling her name. 'We wondered if we could have some tea.'

And his mother, startled, embarrassed, pleased, began to move, darted everywhere. Plates, cups, saucers, fresh tea. 'Why didn't this boy tell me? He's hopeless. You'd like to wash your hands. Dick, fetch a towel; no, I'll do it.'

They ate, sitting opposite each other, tense, embarrassment rising and falling in waves but always, whenever silence seemed about to sweep over their heads for ever, Dick's father found the phrase to split the surface and send words rippling round the table.

It was over; it was even enjoyable; and once, just before they left, Dick's mother was able secretly to snatch at his hand and say, 'She's nice!'

When they came to get their bicycles from the yard, Dick's shame had gone and Helen was happy.

It was dusk. Street lamps winked through the trees on the far side of the park. After the ordeal they were relaxed and when they met Pat and Jim they made fun of Mrs Knowles and Miller.

'It looks to me as though they're going to get married,' said Pat.

'They're suited,' said Dick. 'Her Tom's got some theory about King John's Treasure.'

'Shut up!' said Helen, 'We're not supposed to say.'

'I forgot,' said Dick.

'Tell us, Doddsy.' Jim had found another crack in Dick's armour and would exploit it.

'What am I going to do?' Dick looked at Helen.

'Please yourself.'

Jim laughed. The dilemma was Dick's.

Dick tried to change the subject. 'We didn't tell you what we saw earlier on, did we?' The log in the lane had been lost behind many events.

He told them, but it seemed a thin story. Jim was scornful.

'You certainly know how to make 'em up, Doddsy.'

'Say what you like,' said Dick, 'that wasn't an ordinary bit of wood. It was sea wood. And it was there for a purpose.' He was overstating his case, but he was angry.

'Pull the other one,' said Jim.

'I'll bet you what you like it won't be there tomorrow. I'll bet you what you like it isn't even there now.' His head jutted forward.

'You're on.' Jim was calm, already a winner.

'Come on then, let's go.'

Then the girls began to protest. It was too late and they were beginning to get frightened. But Jim and Dick were on their mettle; no backing down.

To end it, Helen even went back to the start of the disagreement. 'Oh tell him about the blasted Treasure and let's forget about it.'

'I'll tell him,' said Dick. 'And then we'll see about the log.' In some way Miller's theories seemed to back him up. If a solicitor believed that, the log was not so mad. So he told Jim about the Treasure.

'I could have told you that,' said Pat. 'Most of it, anyway. Mrs Shepherd told my mother.'

Jim was chuckling, superior. 'You're mixed up with a right lot,' he said. 'Everybody knows there was no treasure. Everybody except cranks.'

And Dick knew Jim was right. 'It's not treasure I'm interested in, anyway,' he said. 'It's the log.'

'Give it a rest, Doddsy.'

Dick wanted to talk but none of them wanted to hear. And it was time for Helen to be leaving.

'As it's become so dangerous,' said Jim, 'we'll all come and then we can see he gets safely home.'

'What it is to have a friend,' said Dick, but his good humour was returning and deep in his mind he was glad somebody would be with him on the way back.

They left the town behind them, riding two abreast. Pat chattered and Jim laughed. The other two joined in. Courting couples.

With the slow loss of the sun the sky grew pale and the whisper of their wheels held them together. They travelled in a little room drifting further and further into the fens.

'Now we're in Doddsy's country,' said Jim.

'I'm glad I'm not by myself,' said Pat.

The moon put pale fire into a few high clouds and made black shadows run with their wheels. It was a peaceful night and Dick had no fear of it. The river was far away, out of sight.

'What about this log, then?' said Jim. He was teasing Pat.

'No!' she said.

'Forget it,' said Dick. I'll take you to the place tomorrow if you like.' Helen, alongside him, said nothing.

'Scared?' said Jim.

'You can't leave anything alone, can you?' Pat was angry.

'He can't.' Helen backed her up.

'I'm dead scared,' said Dick, refusing to rise to Jim's taunting. But in his own mind he had doubts. Was he scared? Then he decided. Let it go; it didn't matter tonight.

'Thought so,' said Jim. He could not resist it. And Dick fell silent. Ahead of them was the turning that would take them to the lane. Nearer and nearer. It was a test. He knew it and so did Helen. She saw him, head bowed, shut in on himself.

She came up close to him. 'You don't have to,' she said softly.

'No,' he said.

'I know you dare do it,' she said. 'Don't pay any attention to him.'

He could see the turning ahead, a moonlit space, an

invitation. Helen drew away from him slightly. It was up to him.

The space yawned suddenly, he trod hard on his pedals and they were past. It was behind them, and they were riding on. A defeat and a victory. He clenched his teeth. But he was safe for tonight. What did it matter? A weight had gone from him and, as easily as riding downhill, they drifted into Helen's village.

22

It was Pat who had the tact to mention it. Half-way along the drove to Helen's house she said, 'We'll wait for you here.' She made Jim stop and the other two rode alone to her gate.

'When will I see you tomorrow?' Dick asked.

Helen did not give him an answer. 'It took a bit of courage,' she said. 'He was trying to tempt you all the time.'

'Old Jim,' said Dick. 'He's like that. Always pushing you on.'

Helen put her arms round his neck and kissed him. 'That's for being a good boy,' she said. She was happy and relieved. A lot had happened during the day and now they were safe. He even had somebody to see him home.

But as a kiss it was unsatisfactory. A kiss as a reward is no kiss. Now he wanted to kiss her, but she pushed him away. 'Tomorrow,' she said. She made him go.

He rode back down the drove. 'That was quick,' said Pat, and Jim laughed.

Back through the village where the trees drooped heavily over the little houses and all the life of the day had drawn within doors.

'They go to bed early in these parts,' said Jim.

'Let's get home.' Pat felt cold.

They rode faster. It was exhilarating. Clouds, coming up from the horizon, began to crowd the moon, and sometimes now they rode in darkness, their lamps prodding ahead with little yellow rods.

'Wouldn't like to go looking for that thing you saw now,' said Jim. It was a careless remark and meant nothing.

'Scared?' The taunt was Dick's. Revenge.

'No. Cold.'

They were coming to the turning. Dick pushed ahead. 'This way!' he cried.

They were going fast. They had to brake hard to make the corner.

'Where are we going?' Pat's voice was behind him.

'Short cut!'

'Liar!' said Jim.

It was impossible to see the entrance to the lane. The hedges and trees were matted in the darkness. The breeze chilled them, but a deeper shiver told Dick where they were.

'Stop!' They pulled up alongside him. 'This is the place,' he said. 'Coming?' He bent over his handlebars pulling at the lamp to free it.

'You're not right, Doddsy.' Dick heard the quaver in Jim's tone and smiled.

It was Pat who hurt him. 'You promised Helen,' she

said. He was a traitor. But tomorrow he would be forgiven.

Dick laid his bike on the verge and pointed the lamp.

'It's starting to rain!' Pat's voice was already a wail.

'It's only a spot. Won't take a minute. Anybody coming?' He moved towards the lane's dark mouth, waving the beam into it.

Jim threw his bike down. 'Right,' he said. There was hardness in his voice, challenge accepted. And Pat did not dare stay behind. She clung to Jim's hand and they followed.

After a few steps Dick switched off the light.

'What did you do that for?' Pat was startled, almost crying out.

'Quiet!' said Dick. 'I know the way.' And the moon, making rags of the clouds for him, let him see the way ahead.

The rain came to join them, tapping into the leaves.

'Oh!' Pat wailed.

But it suited Dick. Their own noise was hidden.

Jim spoke softly. 'Good place for a murder.' It was bravado. He cackled gently and unconvincingly.

Dick paused. They drew together. He whispered. 'Just up there.' They saw his pointing arm. He knew he was making the others afraid. Let them know what he had been through.

They crept closer. The moon went and came again. The breeze rustled the trees. They stood still. Tense. Dick pointed again. They saw the top bar of the gate.

Closer, foot by foot, the cold grass, unseen, brushing their legs. Dick listened to Pat gasping and forced his lips to smile. Cruel.

The patter of the rain quickened. He glanced up as the moon, wrapped in a heavy cloud, went out for good.

Now. He switched on the light. The beam sprang. The gate seemed to leap at them. Bright. Hard. Clear. And beyond it shadows. Moving? Cold air in their open mouths. Nothing stirred.

Dick lunged forward. Prove the log then go. They were with him, hands holding him as they reached the gate. He stabbed the light at the gate's foot. Look, said the beam.

Nothing but grass. Green grass in the yellow beam.

Was the log on its feet? Ahead of him now? Looking at him? A thin scream of skin and scalp as he searched with the one light, here, there, to and fro, waving it wildly. Nothing.

'It's gone.' His own voice.

And Jim laughed as his blood came back. There was an explanation. There never had been anything there.

'Come on, Doddsy, let's go.'

'Yes,' said Pat. 'I don't like it.' But her fear was also dwindling. Logs of wood. Rubbish. And the rain thickened, drenching down into the standing wheat beyond the gate. Dick's lamp lifted and its beam was shot through with silver streaks as it pointed over the fen.

He swept it across the flat top of the corn. Left to right. A weak thing, reaching no distance. Once more, and he stopped half-way. At the edge of the light, at its very limit. They strained their eyes. A dark shape stood upright in the corn.

Pat was breathing quickly. They both heard her. They both felt the need to protect her.

The beam blurred. A sudden swirl of wind bent the wheat towards them, the whole field moving, and with it the shape strode.

Pat's gasps shuddered up into a scream like a whip in the wind. Legs, arms, as they turned, twisted and locked. They pushed clear and ran. Panic combed the flesh from them and the beam made new shapes jump before them. Like an army from hell they hit the highway, burst on to the road, ran and wrenched up their clumsy bicycles. Once, once only, as he stooped, Dick shone his lamp back the way they had fled. Nothing. Then he was with them.

They slewed at the corner, shattering columns of rain, spray bursting from their wheels, and suddenly they were clear of danger and knew it.

Jim lifted his face to the rain and laughed. Pat had fury burning within her.

'What are you laughing at?' She was bent low, seeking shelter but there was no shelter.

'Doddsy's done it again!' Jim shouted.

'Done what!' She was shrieking at him.

'Scared us with shadows,' said Jim. 'And now we're bloody drenched.'

'There was somebody in the field!' she cried. There had to be or she was being made a fool.

'I'm game to go back and prove there wasn't.'

'In this! You're an idiot!'

And Dick said nothing. Then Jim began to taunt him, insisting he had frightened them with nothing. Dick spoke mildly, agreeing. It was a shadow in the rain.

Soon they were riding grimly, saying nothing, anxious to get home. Pat hated the rain, Jim swore at it, but Dick lingered, falling behind, too wet to get any wetter, not caring.

He was able to part from them before they reached the town and he stood for a while by the roadside, his shirt clinging to his chest, water running down his back, his feet wet and cold. He wanted to be with Helen, alone in the rain, listening to it drenching the fields, changing the smell of the air.

It came again in the night, roaring on the roof, flooding the gutters, and he thought of nothing but Helen.

23

He woke very early, in the thin light. A single sheet lay across him. He pushed it off. The easy weather of summer. He crossed the room to the window and looked out. Barely a single bird call yet. He wanted to be out in the cool air, alone. Why not? He dressed and carefully swung back the bedroom door.

The centre of the house, the staircase, was dim and the still air was warm. He went down stealthily, barefooted. In the kitchen he put on his socks and shoes and turned the key in the back door. It clicked, the door cracked as it opened and he shivered in the cool air as he stood and listened, but no sound came from upstairs. He shut the door behind him softly.

The rain in the night had cleaned everything. Cleaned him himself. Fantasies had been washed from his mind. He had a girl. He would let the wide new morning fill with Helen.

In the backyard, pools still clung to corners, and outside in the street the gutters were wet. He got on his bike and rode, the only traffic, thin-wheeled, in the silent town.

He was in no hurry, he was aiming for no destination, but swiftness was easy. Curtains hung like heavy eyelids in every house, and the empty streets channelled him faster than he thought to the edge of the town. And then he slowed. He was being forced out towards the place they had fled from in the night. No more of that. This was Helen's morning.

He turned in the road. If anyone was watching what would they think? He circled nonchalantly. But that would seem guilty; a youth sauntering before full light, up to no good. He rode away, gathering speed, somebody with an innocent destination. Across the end of the Avenues. A shudder. Damn water-divining. And now he was going down his own road again. He did not look at his own house.

In the middle of the town a milkman with his electric trolley was buzzing and rattling in the market place. Already the loneliness was diminishing.

The bridge. Over it, the wideness of the water like long wings on either side, and he turned to swoop along the brink. Behind him the low sun plated the windows of Mrs Knowles's house with gold. Faster. The road forked like a snake's tongue and he bent to the right away from the river. No houses. Out and clear. This was it, the morning he wanted. No clouds in the sky and he a tiny moving thing beneath it.

The distances grew greater, reminded him of something. A picture of Stonehenge; the plain, the distant stones and shafts of sunlight supporting the clouds. Here there were no clouds, but the quality was the same. He started to sing and a phrase, 'water-colour morning', came into his mind but he kept it from his mouth. They were words for a simpering poem to impress a foolish woman like Mrs Knowles. The road was real and so was the iron bridge over a drainage ditch. He crossed it, going too fast, forced to wrench at the handlebars, concentrating on the road. Just enough risk to make him laugh.

Safe, on a narrow bank. He raised his head. A huge giddiness made him weave and cling to his brakes. Beyond the bank there was no land, only sky. Sky beneath him. The edge of the world. His feet touched earth but he was falling, about to be tipped into space. He clung to useless handlebars and his wild eyes swept in from where there was no horizon towards his feet.

At the bottom of the bank there was water. Water.

He raised his eyes. From where he stood to the horizon it was mirror calm. It put the sky underfoot. But now he saw, away to one side, a thin row of trees, two-faced on the mirror. He slowly swung his head. Far out in the water meadow a group of cattle stood, hanging in nothingness like birds. His eyes took in details. The water was very shallow. Stalks of grass pricked through it in many places. It was only inches deep from the storm of the night before. This was one of those places they let flood; a wash letting where the grass grew lush for grazing.

He breathed deeply, eased his grip on the handlebars and began to ride, sauntering now and letting his imagination put him once again on the causeway at the world's edge. For Helen.

He looked back towards the town. It wrinkled the horizon, black roof-tops and a spire against the rising sun. From this, he had only to turn his head and he was gazing again into nothingness. But now the sun glinted on the water, found a ripple and flashed. Suddenly he knew. He stopped and looked back at the town. The line was right. From a tall house a telescope could have picked him out. He had found Mrs Knowles's Silver Fields.

Off with shoes and socks. Like a kid at the seaside he slid down the wet grass bank and plunged his feet into the cool water. He had forgotten to roll his trousers up. They clung wet round his ankles. He didn't care. He ran, and spray scattered. He stopped and watched the ripples ride away, lengthening and subsiding. He walked. It was like a courtyard flooded for a king's whim. If only Helen could be with him with her feet, like his, in the cool sunken grass. But by mid-morning it would be gone, drained away and dried up by the sun. Get some for her; a piece of silver. How? He ran back and climbed the bank.

In his saddlebag there was a pullover, two spanners, a puncture repair kit. In one side pocket a piece of rag; in the other, nothing.

'But I will take you some of this water!' He spoke aloud. It was an idiot's idea, therefore he was more determined. He emptied the puncture repair tin. There was nothing else.

Once more down the bank and he waded out into the meadow, further than before, out into the purest water, rinsing the oblong tin as he went. Then he filled it, wiped it dry against his shirt and tilted it. Water dripped from under the lid, but very slowly. If he held it level he could take some back.

He dried his feet on his socks, looking out over the lagoon. It was not so mad. He had done crazier things than this. He stood up. 'What do I give you, my Helen?' he said. 'Silver water!'

He looked down at the little yellow tin at his feet and laughed, but he picked it up carefully and, using his pullover, wedged it level in his saddlebag. Then he turned and cycled slowly back to the iron bridge.

The lagoon was lost behind him but the sun was up and the fields were drying, covered in mist that would soon be shimmering and vanishing. The town was waking but it was too early to call on Mrs Knowles.

At home nobody was yet stirring. He found an aspirin bottle that was almost empty, tipped the remaining tablets down the sink, washed the bottle and removed the label. He dried it and then carefully poured in the water from the lagoon and screwed on the cap.

He crept upstairs. On the landing a thin beam of sunlight cut into the house. He held the bottle up to it. Twentieth-century magic phial. But it glinted. Helen might not laugh too much.

His trouser legs were still damp. It didn't matter. He took off all his clothes. He yawned, not sure that he was really tired, but he lay down and pulled up the sheet.

When he woke for the second time it was late. It was mid-morning before he left the house and when he got to the park gate the others were there, even Helen, and he had promised to ride out to meet her.

'Glad you could come,' said Pat.

Dick tried to grin. 'Sorry,' he said to Helen. She barely looked at him.

'You've got last night to apologize for as well,' said Pat. She had the spite of a telltale schoolgirl.

'You're in the dog-house, mate,' said Jim.

'I didn't mean anything to happen last night,' said Dick. Last night was an irritation, a nothing after what had happened this morning.

'Only got us all wet through,' said Pat.

Helen would still not look at him. He had promised not to do anything about the log, and then he had gone off with the others, leaving her out. Dick spoke to her vehemently. 'The log had gone!' he said. 'And there was somebody there, in the field!'

It was Jim's signal. 'You're behind the times, Doddsy. We've worked it all out. A lump of wood and a shadow in the rain. That's all there is to it.'

Dick ignored him. 'The log had gone,' he said to Helen.

'Oh shut up about your stupid old log!' She raised her head as though to stop the tears spilling from her eyes.

'You're on your own, mate,' said Jim.

And Helen found it unbearable. She started to ride away.

'Where are you going?'

She heard Dick's voice behind her. He sounded bewildered. 'Home,' she said. It was difficult to say anything in the anguish that choked her.

Dick started after her up the narrow street away from the gate. Jim was going with him until Pat called him back.

Dick was alongside her. 'I thought of you in the rain,' he said. 'I thought of nothing else.'

It was too public. Two shy people and words like these. But he kept on. 'I woke up thinking about you this morning,' he said, reckless now, except that he looked straight ahead and spoke as though he was talking to himself. 'I went out early,' he said.

'This morning?' Her words were very quiet.

'Dawn. Because I was thinking about you.'

It was unfair. Typical of him, she knew now, to pour out everything, himself, as a gift. It was a sort of arrogance but she could not resist it.

Words did not come easily for her. 'I didn't know,' she said, and fell silent.

Then he told her about what he had found; words, theories, proofs of the Silver Fields. She listened as they rode through the town, knowing where he was heading, and reluctant to go. He was excited. Things had taken a turn for the better, from the dark side of the town they were heading for the light. It was Mrs Knowles again; he was still bound up with her.

'So we shall have to go and tell her,' he said.

'Do we have to?' she said. With Pat and Jim she was on solid ground, but Dick was always pulling her away from land.

'I got you a present,' he said. He laughed at himself.

A present. She blushed.

'I fetched you a bit of the Silver Fields,' he said. 'I've got it in a bottle at home.'

She laughed with him. 'Honestly,' she said, 'you are a fool!'

When they got to the house on the brink there was no answer to the doorbell. They tried the back gate. It was bolted.

Dick was dejected but Helen, relieved at missing another ordeal in the big house, teased him. 'I know where she is,' she said. 'She's out with her man.'

She had said the wrong thing. It gave him an idea. 'Bet you're right,' he said. 'Let's go and see if she's at Miller's!'

'We can't. You know he thinks this is all a lot of non-sense.'

'But she might be with him.'

Helen sighed. 'All right,' she said. 'But if she's not there that's the end of it.'

'Very well. It's a bargain. Then I'll take you home and give you the precious phial of silver water.'

'Thank you very much.'

They dawdled across the town. The day was bright and the sun had sucked up most of the effects of the overnight storm, thickening the air in the market place, but in the Avenues the trees clung to the coolness and the grass beneath them was still damp. The hedges along Miller's drive, like sponges, held water within them, but the house itself, unshielded, caught the full glare of the sun and seemed dried out and brittle. And it was empty.

Helen turned to go. It was her day. No more alarms.

'Just let's look round the back,' said Dick. 'They might be out in the garden or something.'

He had to go to the limit. It was a point of honour with him. She knew it, and together they walked round the corner of the house to the garden. It was still a colour photograph on a calendar. They went past the french windows, taking sidelong glances into the room. It was empty as far as they could see.

'Come on,' said Helen, 'let's go.' Being an interloper made her nervous, but Dick saw what seemed to be a greenhouse jutting beyond the far side of the house.

'They might be in there,' he said. It was as far as he intended to go, a tiny dare.

'But they wouldn't like us looking in on them,' she said.

'Speak louder,' he said, 'then it won't seem like we're snooping around.' He walked forward, making as much noise with his feet as he could and saying something to her over his shoulder. Something about the weather.

The greenhouse turned out to be a conservatory built against the end of the house, but as a sun-trap it was spoiled by the shrubs that grew tall and close to it, and made it dim inside. A quiet, green place. He liked it and wanted to see inside. And one more dare made him smile. He would kiss her there, in Miller's garden.

As they approached it was clear there was nobody inside, but Dick took Helen's hand to take her right up to the glass. There they would be hidden in the shrubs. He stopped and put his arm around her.

'No!' she said. 'Not here.' She was pushing him away.

He laughed and, holding both her hands, began to draw her into the shade of a tall bush that almost touched the glass.

Helen was reluctant but she went with him. Then they could go.

Two paces. He was stepping backwards. Behind him she saw the shelves of geranium pots on the other side of the glass, white chairs and an iron table with curling florid legs.

He was looking into her face. Her large dark eyes were apprehensive. He smiled because he had the power to calm them. But she was not looking at him; she was afraid they would be seen. The glass room behind him was empty. He knew it was. If anybody was coming it would be through the garden and he would see them first. Still her eyes would not come to his. And suddenly they did not belong to him. Fear grew in them. Her nails dug hard into his palms. She held so tightly he could turn nothing but his head.

The tables and chairs stood where they were in the green light. Everything was peaceful, at rest. Then he saw what made her cling to him.

It lay on the floor. A roll of carpet. No. A shape within the carpet. Wrapped up like a body. A body in a green glass mausoleum.

Dick felt the coldness of the mud, and knew what had found its way to Miller's house.

Speak. Make words. But most of all get away.

They stepped back from the mausoleum, treading the bushes, pushing into branches that pressed against them like thin arms that wanted to send them back. And to their right, at the garden's edge, a gate opened in the high wooden fence and Miller stepped through.

They stopped. They watched him. He was like some thin animal in a forest. But he did not see them. He turned to shut the gate, stooped to bolt it and for a moment was out of sight.

Hide or run? Dick tugged Helen's hand, pulling her with him away from the conservatory. They might get away unseen. Miller stood up, still with his back to them, to shoot home another bolt. They walked away from him softly. And then he turned. Helen jerked at Dick's arm. Run. She wanted to run. But Dick held firm. Face him in the open.

He saw them. A frown, no more; and from beneath the heavy eyebrows the small eyes stabbed from one to the other and calculated. A decision was made. He came to-wards them calmly, and he was smiling, but his eyes were continuously flickering away from them, searching for something.

Innocence was necessary. Dick let go of Helen's hand. 'Hello, Mr Miller,' he said, 'we were just . . .'

'Where is Mrs Knowles?' Miller thought she was with them. He paid them little attention.

'We thought she might be here. We were looking for her.' An innocent answer and an explanation.

'What!'

Eyes and voice together lunged at him.

'She's not at home,' said Dick. His mouth was dry.

'I know that. Where is she?' Miler was stepping quickly towards them, menacing.

'I don't know.' Dick moved half a step as though to stand between Helen and Miller, and Miller pulled up short.

His voice was smooth, a lawyer's slippery trap. 'Then why are you here?' A pause. 'In my garden?'

His garden. It was an accusation. Unjust. Helen heard anger flickering in Dick's voice. 'I told you.'

He was daring too much. She broke in. 'We rang the bell but nobody came. We thought you might be round the back.'

'You've just this instant arrived?'

She nodded. And it was then, for the first time, that Miller looked towards the conservatory. A quick glance and then back to them. He seemed to relax. He put his head back. 'My word, it's hot again,' he said.

He began to shepherd them towards the house, and Dick, as he turned, also looked at the conservatory. The floor and what lay on it were out of sight.

Without talking they went to the front of the house.

They were being turned out. They reached their bicycles.

'If you see Mrs Knowles,' said Miller, 'tell her I also would like to see her.' He spoke casually. They were ready to go. 'And one more thing.' They looked up at him. He raised his eyebrows, smiling, making a joke. 'Don't let us have any more nonsense.'

It was not far to the road. They were within easy reach of safety.

'What do you mean?' said Dick.

'I do not care for your truculent tone, young man!'

'Then tell us what you mean!' Dick's fury made Helen's heart leap.

Miller's mouth shut tight. He drew in his breath so sharply his nostrils narrowed. For a second he seemed about to come at them, but he held himself upright and spoke with sharp anger. 'Mrs Knowles is in a state of strong nervous tension. You, Mr Dodds, are well aware of that! You, Mr Dodds, have had a great deal to do with it! If you say as much as one word to her about that fiasco of the log you shall have to answer for it to me! Now good day to you both!'

He turned from them swiftly and strode towards the door. Dick's cheek muscles bunched. He was going to fight. Helen pushed into him. Barged into him. Anything to stop him.

'Dick! Come with me! I've got something to tell you!' The words were in his ear as his eyes glared. The words won. Savagely he turned, kicked gravel, and with her thrust the house and Miller behind him.

24

But she had no idea in her mind; nothing to tell him. It didn't matter; his own mind was full of humiliation and he rode alongside her, his head lowered, his lips thin and savage, full of contempt for himself.

'Stop it,' she said.

'Stop what!'

'Stop thinking about it.'

'I hate that swine!' He imitated Miller. '"Kindly get off the premises." And he meant you too. Doesn't it make you want to go back and rip into him?' He turned to her, head like an eagle's except it was he who was feeling the pain.

'No,' she said. 'I don't care.'

She wore a white dress on which little blue flowers were scattered. She was smaller than himself, softer, a victim. And he could never despise a victim.

'Where are we going?' she said.

'I don't know. Anywhere we can think.' He was trembling slightly. 'What was it you were going to tell me?'

She let her mind clutch at anything. 'Give me my present,' she said.

'What?'

'The bottle of magic water.'

And then he understood he had been tricked.

'You little devil!' he said.

But she had won, and he was almost laughing.

'You promised,' she said.

He was laughing now. 'I haven't got it. It's at home.'

'Then take me there.' She held his eyes.

'Very well.'

He took her along the quieter roads; the middle of the town would be full of the risk of meeting people he knew. And there was something else in his mind; the important thing. 'Well, anyway,' he said, 'there's one thing we've discovered. Miller has the log.'

The shape wrapped in the carpet. The incident seemed far away; the confrontation with Miller was like a wall between them and it.

'Dick,' she said, 'It wasn't anything. Anybody can have a rolled-up carpet in an outhouse.'

'But I felt it,' he said. 'The feeling of the mud. I know it was there.'

'You know too much,' she said. 'It's always getting you into trouble.' Without looking at him she heard him sigh and she knew he was giving way to her. 'Be sensible, Dick. We know what Mrs Knowles is like. Yesterday she thought water-divining solved everything. Who knows what she thinks today? And that man was worried about her. He wouldn't do anything to frighten her.'

'It was there,' he said flatly. 'I felt it.'

But he had doubts now, and she sensed them. 'We were both jumpy,' she said.

They were near his house and he was thinking about taking her into it. He said nothing. There was nobody at home. He relaxed.

'I'll make you a cup of coffee,' he said.

Helen, slightly nervous in his home again, nodded.

'At least,' he said, 'I will if you give me a kiss for it.'

'That's all you think about,' she said.

'Nothing else is ever in my mind. Nothing.'

'I don't know that I want to be in a mind like yours.'

He laughed. 'You can't help it. You're in and the doors are shut and I'll never let you go.'

He kissed her. Her eyes closed, the long dark eyelashes quivering down until they seemed to touch her cheeks. He held her close and pushed his face into her hair. 'I don't know who's captured who,' he said.

Her hands against his shoulders began gently to push him away. 'What if your mother comes in?' she said.

'Don't care.'

But she insisted. 'I want my coffee and I want my present.'

'I don't know why I like you,' he said. 'I've never met anybody so mercenary.'

'You don't know anything about fen people. Real fen people.'

He filled the kettle and showed her where the cups were.

'Now I'll fetch you some bottled magic,' he said.

She heard him running up the stairs. He paused and listened for her getting out the cups and saucers. She was timid, making very little noise. He sang as he ran up to his bedroom, and a few moments later he was with her again in the kitchen.

'Here you are,' he said. 'From the Silver Fields!'

He held out the aspirin bottle and they both began to laugh.

'Isn't it magnificent?' he said. 'Nobody has ever had a gift like that.'

She took it, a little bottle with a white screw top. It was stupid, but she wanted to cry.

'Kettle's boiling,' he said. He set about making the coffee.

While his back was towards her she looked at the bottle and then she put it in the pocket of her dress. They did not mention it again.

They sat at the kitchen table.

'You know,' he said, 'there is this new mystery.'

'What's that?'

'The disappearance of Mrs Knowles.'

Mrs Knowles again. 'If she was your mother you wouldn't be talking about her all the time!' The words came out quickly and she was ashamed of them. They hit him hard. Why did he have to be so sensitive? 'Sorry,' she said, 'but I'm fed up with hearing about her.'

Her head was down. Like a little bull. He liked her to menace him.

'I think you're safe from her,' he said. 'She's wrapped up in a carpet in Miller's conservatory.'

Helen shuddered. 'You've got a horrible mind,' she said.

They drank their coffee.

'But we ought to find her,' said Dick, 'and tell her about the Silver Fields.' Silver Fields, the words sounded stupid, like a trade name, but Mrs Knowles had invented it. 'It would put her mind at rest.'

'Mr Miller wouldn't be very pleased.'

'To hell with him! I'm going to find her.'

Arguing was useless and Helen knew it. 'But where are we going to look?'

He hadn't a single idea and being pinned down was an irritation. 'I don't know. Why don't we go and see our old witch? She's been involved.'

Mrs Shepherd. The idea had come from nowhere. At least it was something to do. But would Helen come? He looked at her carefully.

'All right.' She was calm.

'Are you humouring me?' He was half-glowering, half-smiling.

'Yes.'

They made a detour to avoid the park and came into the little street from the far end. It made it worse for Helen; she had not realized how deeply embedded among houses they had been on their first visit. They turned into street after street, wriggling into a mass of red brick, airless and barren except for the children roaming in groups. They paid her no attention but she felt afraid of them as though they would suddenly, in a gang, turn on her.

Dick slowed, examining the houses. 'What number was it?' he said.

'Is this the street?' She could not even recognize it.

'It's along here somewhere,' he said. 'I wouldn't like to call at Pat's by mistake.'

Suddenly Helen started. Close beside her someone was rapping at a window, but unseen, rapping on the glass through a net curtain. The curtain itself pecked at the glass, rap, rap, rap. Then someone was scrabbling at it, bunching it up from the bottom, and from under a tent of lace the round face of Mrs Shepherd was leering.

Dick smiled and waved and pointed to the archway at the side of the house, and the head nodded and smiled and the curtain dropped back into place.

'She made me jump,' said Helen. Her heart was thumping.

'Bit of luck,' said Dick. 'Bet I'd have gone to the wrong place.'

They were through the tunnel and the gate by the time Mrs Shepherd was opening the back door.

'I gave you a fright, dear,' she said to Helen. 'You look all pale and flummoxed. Come you on in and sit down.'

In the cramped, dark room it was cool.

'Can I get you a nice cup of tea?' The old woman was fussing round them.

'No thanks,' said Dick. 'We've just had one.'

Mrs Shepherd ignored him. It was as though their last meeting had never happened. 'Can I, dear?' she said to Helen.

'No thank you, Mrs Shepherd.'

Mrs Shepherd wore a long apron over her black dress. 'I've just been getting my dinner ready,' she said.

In the front room? The question was in Dick's head. He said nothing, but Mrs Shepherd looked at him sharply before she added, still speaking to Helen, 'I've been keeping my eye on the front. Something's happening.' Once again the little gleam of secret power. 'But sit you down.' She mothered Helen into a chair and let Dick fend for himself.

'Were you coming to me for any special reason?' she said.

'Well,' said Helen, uncertainly.

Mrs Shepherd interrupted. 'Never mind whether you were or whether you weren't, I've got something to tell you. A lady was here only just this morning and she was asking about you. Oh, poor soul, she was in a state. Looked as though she's been out in all weathers, like a diddecoy, except that you could tell she wasn't.'

'Who was it?' Dick's voice rang out in the gloom.

'Why do you ask, boy? You know who it was.' Again the dislike in her voice. But her next words were meant for him even though she still spoke to Helen.

'You're mixed up in something very strange, aren't you, dear?' Helen nodded. 'And you don't like it, do you?'

'No.' Helen's voice was no more than a whisper.

'But that boy friend of yours is having the time of his life, and don't let him tell you different.'

Helen's face was in shadow but he knew she took her eyes from Mrs Shepherd to look at him. As she did so, Mrs Shepherd leant forward to pat her hand. 'Don't worry, lovey. He ain't so bad. Just a bit extreme and I don't want you getting into no danger. But you've got a good little head on your shoulders, I can see that, so I'll tell you what happened.'

'Can't Dick listen?' She still spoke in a whisper.

'He can, but I'm telling you.'

There was a pause as she dug into her apron pocket for a handkerchief. She took off her glasses, polished them, and put them back on.

'Now this lady had heard about me – I dare say you can guess from who – and she came to see me because of the trouble she's in all through that damn foolishness of King John's Jewels. Damned old rubbish! They never did exist, did they?' This to Dick, sharply.

'No,' he said.

'At least you've got *some* sense.' She turned back to Helen. 'Well this lady got mixed up in it in a similar way to you dear. And like I nearly did, only I could see which way it was leading. But that Mr Miller, he's like this one here,' she nodded her head towards Dick, 'he won't be put off and he takes her down to that bad place near the river mouth, takes her down there again after all my warnings, poor thing, and she still in a state after losing her poor husband. Oh, you men, you make me mad!'

Dick stayed silent, wondering if the old woman would ever get to the point. Suddenly she was speaking savagely.

'Where did the idea of the body come from?'

'You know as well as I do,' said Dick.

'That I do! He's a fool, that man! He don't believe it no more than I do, but it's got hold of her mind, poor thing, and now she thinks the thing is walking. Walking, if you please; following her!'

The little room was very cold and the furniture was black except for the white eye of the mirror, blank and pitiless.

'Why her?' said Dick. 'Why her and not Miller?'

There was real anxiety in his voice, and Mrs Shepherd relented. When she spoke again she included him.

'Now that I don't know,' she said. 'The poor thing's mind is in such a muddle. But he put it into her head, that I do know. He's responsible. If he hadn't gone interfering, none of this would have happened. None of it. And now she's sure that when this thing gets to her house, she'll die.'

'Oh!' Helen's hands went to her mouth.

'Now don't take on. It's all in her imagination like I explained the other day to this boy friend of yours. There's nothing coming in from the sea to kill her. Such nonsense! I put her mind at rest, I have that power too, you know. Lots of people come to old Mother Shepherd when they're in trouble.'

There was pride in her voice. She sat plump and safe in her tiny dark room and believed she could work wonders.

'Dear, you look faint. This business is all a bit too much.'

And you are making it worse, you old witch, Dick thought.

Helen could not answer. It was up to Dick. He had his hands on his knees; his shoulders hunched. Should he tell her what they knew? All of it? What he said was, 'Could the log walk, do you think?'

Mrs Shepherd's reaction was violent. 'Boy, are you an idiot!' It was almost a shout. 'Of course it can't!'

The fat little woman was a ball of fury. Real danger, real fear had touched her and she was fighting it off. Useless to tell her anything. Calm her down.

'No,' he said. 'Of course not. If it is coming inland somebody is carrying it.'

'You are a fool!' She was still almost shouting. 'Nothing is coming inland. It's all in the poor creature's imagination as I told her. And if you go disturbing her with any more of your tales I will hound you and hound you until you'll wish you'd never been born. Do you hear me?'

Another warning. First Miller, now the old woman. They had to get out. Helen was trembling, beginning to sway. He stood up.

'I'm sorry, Mrs Shepherd,' he said. His voice was very clear. At that moment he was unafraid. 'I won't do anything to harm her, I promise.'

The little woman was beginning to look ill. 'I know, I know,' she said. 'You're a good young man at heart. You just take the wrong things too seriously sometimes. Don't mind me yelling at you.'

'It's all right, I don't mind. But do you know where Mrs Knowles has gone?'

'Home, I suppose, for a good lay down like I told her. No disturbing her now.' She was suspicious.

'We won't.'

At last they got out. Out into the thick air. Helen felt sick and too weak to ride. She walked beside Dick as he pushed both bicycles away from the little house and the narrow streets, anywhere she could breathe.

25

'You look as though you've seen a ghost!' It was commonplace; it was what they needed. Pat was concerned, but she was also giggling.

And Jim, sitting on the gate, stopped whistling to say to Helen, 'Has he been taking you up green lanes again to show you something nasty?'

Pat's wide mouth opened to let the laughter burst out. 'Isn't he terrible?'

'We ain't all like you, Jimmy boy,' said Dick.

'Damn sight worse,' said Jim. 'I'm going up no lanes with you, Doddsy. Not after last night.'

'You *do* look pale,' Pat was probing, wanting to know what had happened. 'Are you all right?'

'I am now,' said Helen.

Her voice was uncertain. Dick protected her. 'We've been to see the old witch who lives down your road,' he said.

'Oh no!' Pat was shocked. 'Not again. Why?'

'Well.' Dick looked at Jim whose face was blank. 'We were looking for Mrs Knowles.'

'Oh?' Jim raised his eyebrows to put wrinkles across his forehead. Perfect innocence.

'She's missing,' said Dick. 'Or at least she was, but she turned up at Mrs Shepherd's this morning. We must've just missed her.'

'So what happened?' Pat was eager.

Dick looked away. It was going to be difficult. He told them half the story, leaving out Miller, leaving out the Silver Fields. 'It's just that she thinks something from the mud is chasing her,' he said.

'This log thing that she got you to believe in?' said Jim.

'That's right.'

'This log which has vanished?'

Dick nodded.

'This log which never was there anyway?'

'Have it your own way,' said Dick.

'You know what's going to happen?' said Jim.

'Tell me.'

'They're going to have to drag the river for your Mrs Knowles.'

'Jim!' Pat shouted. 'Shut up! You're morbid.'

'Sooner or later,' said Jim.

There was a hideous inevitability in what he said. It froze all Dick's words.

'She won't.' Helen's voice was very quiet but firm. The paleness of her cheeks gave force to her determination.

For a moment, Jim was silenced, then he said, 'How do you know?' There was a trace of the jeer he used against Dick in his voice.

'Because we are not going to let it happen.' She took him seriously and she refuted him. Even if it was just, it was cruel. He had been joking to comfort her, but she rejected him utterly and it hurt. Dick saw it and tried to heal the wound by Jim's own method.

'That's done him,' he said. It was an invitation for Jim to counter-attack, and, in a half-hearted way, he responded. He gave his little cackling laugh but his face was red and a moment later he was whistling and looking at the ground.

'It's hot,' said Pat. 'Let's go somewhere.' She was trying to put all the nonsense behind them, smooth things over.

'We've got to find Mrs Knowles,' said Helen. She was as cold as marble. In a moment Pat would also take offence.

Everything was jarring. Dick tried to bring them together. 'All right,' he said. 'She's probably home by now. Coming with us?'

It depended on Jim. Pat was watching him. He stopped whistling. 'Tell us what happened when you get back,' he said. His face was not unfriendly.

'You're scared,' said Dick.

'After last night, mate, I am.'

'See you, then.'

Dick and Helen rode away.

'Does he have to make fun of everything?' said Helen.

'You know Jim.'

After a moment she said, 'Was I nasty to him?'

'No. Anyway he deserved it.'

'I'll go back and apologize.' She slowed, ready to turn.

'No you won't. They'd only feel obliged to come with us and we don't want them this time.'

'I hate offending people.'

'Don't worry about it. We'll see him later.'

But it was still on her mind when they came to the house on the brink. It was empty, locked front and back as she knew it would be. She knew it in the same way that she had contradicted Jim. A deadly certainty was in her. A climax was coming. This was her day and she was going to see it through.

They were standing in the road at the back of the house when they heard the chimes of the Institute clock. It was noon. The sun high overhead, the traffic in the town sparse and lethargic. The dead time of the day, and it took Dick by surprise.

'You'll never be able to get home in time for dinner,' he said.

'Doesn't matter, I'll give my mother a ring.'

'Have some with us.' Inviting her was becoming both more and less embarrassing. His mother had met her, that made it easy, but soon she would be talking of things getting 'serious' between him and Helen.

26

They needed the interlude. His mother was flustered when they arrived, but pleased as well. And his father was there, so at least the conversation would rest in easy formalities. It did so, until they sat down.

They were just beginning to eat when his mother said,

'Mrs Knowles was round here looking for you this morning, Dick.' She said it with satisfaction. Her son had made an impression.

'How long ago?' He spoke urgently.

'Oh the middle of the morning. She's very nice isn't she?'

They had been in the house during the morning. They must have just missed her.

'What did she want?' This time his tone got through to her.

'Is there anything wrong?' Her quick little head darted like a bird's, from him to Helen and back again. 'She didn't really say. Something about your class and some books.'

'Nothing wrong,' he said. 'We've been looking for her, that's all.'

There were going to be questions. His mother suspected trouble, but his father saw awkwardness looming and did his duty. 'I expect you will meet up with her this afternoon,' he said.

'She looked very nervous,' said his mother.

'She always is,' said Dick. He took a lesson from his father. 'She lost her husband only last year, you know.'

His mother was distressed. 'Oh! And I didn't know.' Now she was wondering if her own behaviour had been correct. The diversion had worked, cruelly, but the interlude was already over. A crisis was coming, and they had to sit and eat and talk about other things.

They escaped as soon as they could and went out. They found themselves going towards the park gate; it seemed like the base for all their operations.

'But I reckon it's too early for anybody else to be there,' said Dick.

He was right. It was siesta time, the trees holding out heavy branches to cast deep shade, and the deserted grass sunning itself. For a while they said nothing. This was the interlude they had been seeking.

'Enjoying yourself?' said Dick.

'I am now. In a way.' She found it strange.

'Well we're getting somewhere,' he said. 'Either somebody is frightening the wits out of Mrs Knowles or she's a bit mad.'

'Or we are.'

He looked at her. She was smiling to herself, secretly.

'I'm mad,' he said, 'but I didn't think you were.'

'More than you think.' She had the bottle of silver water in her pocket. It was warm now. He had given it to her; she had made it warm.

He was leaning over the gate. He pushed himself upright, drawing in his breath and thrusting his fingers through his hair.

'It's losing her husband that's brought all this on. I'm sure of it,' he said.

'But what about Mr Miller?' She did not look at him.

'Well I thought at one time he was a bit sinister,' he said.

A bit, she thought, that was putting it mildly.

'But he did seem to be worried about her this morning,' he said, and laughed. 'Do you know, at one time I thought he was frightening her to death to get her money or something. He is a lawyer.'

She smiled at him. 'Dick, you're crazy! Just because a man's a lawyer. She likes him, didn't you know that? Really likes him.'

Well why didn't she go and see him? Tell me that?

Why did she go and see Mrs Shepherd who hates him? Why did she try to see me?'

There were no answers to those questions. Except that deep down, in her secret self, Helen felt some unguessable impossibility stirring. It could not come into words, and she sat on the gate in silence.

Dick had made his point. Now they needed action. 'Let's go and see if she's home now,' he said.

'Ring her up,' said Helen.

'Why didn't I think of that before?'

'Because you're not very practical.'

They crossed the empty park, the sun burning their shadows into the soft tar of the path, and found a phone box. The telephone made its double buzz mechanically, on and on like an echo of the bell ringing out in the empty house. No answer. It seemed obvious from the beginning.

Dick put the phone down. He was at a loss.

Helen said, 'Why not try Mr Miller?'

'What, and get told off again?'

'I'll do it then. I haven't quarrelled with him.'

She saw Dick bite his lip. He wanted to let her do it. She reached for the phone.

'No,' he said. He would not shelter behind her. Some of the colour had gone from his cheeks. He had a nice mouth, she thought, but now he pressed his lips together tightly and she knew some desperate idea was forming in his head.

'Let me ring him,' she pleaded. 'He won't be nasty with me.'

It was too late. Gently he eased her out of the box. 'We are going to see him,' he said. 'We are going to have it out.'

He was afraid, it was easy to see that, but she did not try to stop him. Was it a dare he had set himself, or this time was it courage? She could not be sure.

It was not far to Miller's house and he made them ride quickly. They came into the silence of the Avenues from the direction of the park. Miller's house was nearer the farther end. He slowed a little. 'The heat!' he said.

Slower still as they neared the gap into the drive.

'Right?' He glanced at her.

She nodded.

They pulled up and got off their bicycles, leaning them against the hedge outside. Dick felt his arms trembling and he was muttering, calling himself a coward.

'What?' said Helen.

'Nothing.'

Then suddenly they both jumped. The black snout of a car pushed out from the driveway entrance and all they heard was the bushes scraping and rattling on its sides. It passed them and paused at the kerb, its engine muttering as the driver glanced quickly up and down the road. No traffic in the whole length of the Avenues. The car growled away, gathering speed. Miller had gone, leaving them standing there.

They looked at each other, startled, then put their hands against each other's shoulders and laughed.

'Wherever the action is today,' said Dick, 'there we aren't!'

'We're pretty useless,' she said.

'You're pretty and I'm useless,' he said and then, quickly, 'No I'm not. Come on.'

He looked up and down the Avenues. The long cave still

slumbered. Dick snatched Helen's hand and pulled her after him into the driveway.

'No!' She was afraid.

'Yes. Suppose he's left her here alone.'

There was no other car in the open space by the front door, but she may have got there by some other means. They stood in the porch and Dick pressed the bell. They heard chimes sounding musically inside. Not loud enough. Dick hammered the knocker.

'Making sure,' he said.

Helen was shrinking away. 'I don't like it.'

The knocking stopped, the chimes died, the house was in silence. Dick looked through the letter box. The hallway was neat and empty.

'Not a soul at home,' he said. He spoke quietly, thinking, and Helen felt worse. She tugged at him. 'Let's go.'

He stepped back from the door, but slowly. 'Now's our chance,' he said. 'I wonder where he keeps the key to that glasshouse.'

'We can't do that!' Helen was panicking. Burglary was far beyond anything she dared do.

He calmed her. 'All right. But just let's go and have one more peep at that carpet. Through the window.' He smiled to put her mind at rest, but there was more in his smile than that. There was a glint.

He did not bother to walk quietly. He blatantly looked through the french windows and only when they were approaching the conservatory did he begin to be cautious. But even then there seemed to be a kind of excited gaiety in him.

'One thing we know, anyway,' he said. 'It's not Mrs

Knowles rolled up in there.' He gave her a devil's grin over his shoulder.

'You're frightening me,' she said. And she was beginning to feel angry.

They came up to the glass together. The white chairs and table in the green gloom, and there, on the stone floor in exactly the same place, the rolled-up carpet.

'Now are you satisfied?'

He did not answer.

'Carpet,' she said. 'A roll of carpet.'

He still had his face against the glass.

'Come on,' she said. 'If it was what you thought it was you'd feel it. The trail and all that.'

'I'm just wondering,' he said, 'if I do feel anything or not.' He was full of sensations; the strange garden, risk-taking. If he felt the cold of the trail he could be deluding himself. He lifted his eyes from the carpet that may or may not contain something. 'There's a door on the other side,' he said. 'Let's try it.'

'No.' She meant it.

He released her hand. 'I'll just go and see. Don't run away.'

A path of paving stones led to the back gate and divided to go around to the back of the conservatory. When he reached the split in the path he felt the chill and was certain, but Helen knew nothing. She saw him through two layers of glass. She saw his hand reach for the door handle. She saw the handle turn inside the summer-house as he tried it, and she saw the door move inwards. She hated the carelessness of Miller in not locking the door. She hated Dick for not raising his eyes to her.

He moved slowly in the green light. As slowly as a fish.

He waded through the air until his feet came to the end of the roll. The other end pointed directly at her. He bent stiffly, both pale arms descending like the rods of a machine. His white fingers closed on the carpet and turned the roll once so that part of the pattern lay flat on the floor. Turkish. A fringe, then little zigzags. The unrolling went on mechanically. Half a turn. The roll was still fat yet already the other fringe showed itself.

He held the loose fringe and lifted it back.

From the flowers on the shelves around him flies leapt and swam down through the green air to the smooth black blot on the carpet. Smooth as a mummy in its shell, wrapped as tight as a black chrysalis, the log lay on the ceremonial zigzags, still with the sea sheen on the weed that clung like hair to the round head over which he was bent. The weed reached to narrow shoulders, sea worn, and the log tapered to a jagged point where the mud had sucked its softer parts away.

In Miller's house. The house rose above her. She saw the log within it. The horror marched on her.

And a car door slammed.

Like pain, the sound pulled Helen's head away from the glass. There was nothing behind her, she was well shielded, but she heard feet crunch gravel at the front of the house.

She moved tenderly. She was aware of the swift, accurate placing of her feet as she ran to the glass door. Dick had not moved. His crouch clamped him close to the log. She went quickly up behind him and stooped to put her hands under his armpits. She heaved. He was like a dead weight until he began to move and then he came up with her, easily.

She stepped to the foot of the log. He stood where he

was. His eyes were dull, but they were on her, obedient. When she stooped to cover the log he bent with her. She smelt the mud reek, she felt the chill of the black thing. Quickly she flung the carpet over it and his hand followed the motion of hers. She stepped to the centre and pushed, rolling the log along the floor. It was easy, lighter than she thought.

Sounds. Now she could hear sounds beyond the door that led into the house. Dick was standing, dazed. She ran and snatched his hand, dragged him outside, pulled the door shut behind her and plunged with him out along the path.

The back gate was double bolted. No time for that. She crashed with him into the bushes, crouched and edged deeper. Then she stopped. Her breathing was heavy, but Miller was still in the house, out of earshot. She could see him through the french windows, a tall grey shape walking to and fro close to the window but never looking out. He was talking but they were too far away to hear any words. There must be somebody with him.

Helen strained her eyes but the depths of the room were too dark. Miller was talking hard and fast, holding himself stiffly but making quick little gestures, arguing a case. Suddenly something at the back of the room moved, but Miller darted, blocking her view. And then he was coming backwards towards the window rocking from side to side. An arm came up to strike him but his hand reached and held the wrist before the blow fell. Its force made him twist, and Helen saw Mrs Knowles fighting; struggling and striking out.

Her own hand wrenched at Dick's and a new fear surged in her. In an instant he would be away from her, out in the open, charging in to the rescue. She held him. Stop him. But there was no need; his hand in hers was lifeless. She tore her eyes from the window. He was not even watching. His face was calm, aware of nothing, and the double fear made her whimper.

A roar from Miller. The sound of a blow. She saw Mrs Knowles, her head hanging back, about to fall. Then Miller caught her and held her. Very slowly her head came up, eyes still closed. Helen winced. Mrs Knowles rested her head against Miller's chest. His arms went round her. He was comforting her.

Helen looked back at Dick. The same terrible lifelessness. Now all she could do was think of him. She held his hand and he followed. She forced her way through the shrubs all the way round the garden, pausing to look at the window, but the two figures clung together without moving.

They came out into the drive beyond Miller's car and stepped into the Avenues.

27

She was safe. Their bikes, pushed into the hedge, were almost out of sight. Miller, as he drove in, could hardly have noticed them. But Dick's hand was still cold in hers. All of her attention was on him. She stood in front of him and was terrified. He was glazed. Not only his eyes, but the skin of his face and of his hand. An absolute calmness possessed him and made him a china figure.

She shook his arm. 'Dick! Look at me!'

His obedient, automatic eyes moved to her. Brown with tawny flecks, the imperfections put in by a craftsman to make his doll lifelike.

She tried to smile at him. He also smiled. A new smooth expression on a perfect doll.

She wanted to cling to him, warm him, bring him back to life. No. She held herself back. The log had done this to him. She also had touched the log. A difference. She fought for the answer. He believed in the evil of it. She fell short of that, failed always in every way to go as far as he did; the trail it left, the dark side of the river and the light side. She did not measure up, couldn't believe. And he had been out at dawn, while she still slept, thinking of her, fetching her a crazy gift of dawn water.

She let her head fall forward, the sign of despair, but she knew as she did it that she was plunging into his world. She had taken from him the silver water. Her hand went to her pocket and closed on the little bottle.

'Dick,' she said. She held the bottle up before his face. No sign of life yet. She did not expect it. She put the bottle in the breast pocket of his shirt. 'We are going away,' she said.

She turned and pulled their bicycles from the hedge. 'Can you ride?'

'Yes.' A word at last.

'Let's go then.' Like a nurse with a patient she went with him, riding outside, protecting him from the traffic.

She took him out of the town, away from it, her way towards her country.

28

Through the long afternoon the long lanes murmured. From horizon to horizon nothing was hidden. She let it work, watching over him, saying nothing.

She looked for her village. Far away the church spire showed through the hump of trees. The sleeping dog had pricked up an ear.

Suddenly Dick stiffened and shuddered. He looked about him, out away across the flat land.

'It was pretty terrible,' he said.

He knew what had happened. But how much of it? She wanted to ask, but he was not yet ready to talk.

'I like the fens,' he said. 'I'd like to live out here. You know where you are.'

She contradicted him to get a response. 'Not in the winter, you wouldn't.'

'Yes I would. You can always see a long way.'

It was enough. She stayed silent. He might still be tender even though he had cracked through the glaze of shock. For a while he said nothing, then he faced her.

'Well, we found the log,' he said. 'I knew Miller was mixed up in it.'

Not a word about the way she had rescued him. Did he know about it, or was he too ashamed of his helplessness to mention it? She was disappointed; she deserved something.

Then he made her heart thump so that the blood roared in her ears and she was dizzy. 'But we've still got to find Mrs Knowles,' he said.

He knew nothing. An hour had gone; a blank page where she had done all the writing while he slept.

'Why are we going this way?' he said.

'Because you like it.' She spoke mechanically.

He was puzzled now, beginning to realize he had missed something. 'We won't find her out here, will we?' he asked. He thought they were following a clue.

'No. We've already found her.' It came out quickly. She told him everything, and they rode slower as though her words were loading a weight in his mind that he could hardly bear.

'The end bit,' he said. 'Tell me the end bit again.'

'Where he hit her?'

'No. You don't know if he did that. You couldn't see.' He had absorbed every detail. 'The last thing we saw.'

We saw. He was coming out of a dream.

'She was crying on his shoulder,' she said.

He frowned. He could not understand it. She feared he would slide into some new wildness.

'Don't you see?' she said. 'It's something between them. None of our business. Why don't we just let them get on with it?'

'I don't know.' He was uncertain.

'Why don't you come to mine for tea?' she said. She wanted her feet on the ground; all their feet on the ground.

'All right.'

She was still nursing him; still in charge. She made him ride faster, made him talk about anything except what they had just seen. She would not let him escape from her, back into his nightmare, and she succeeded. In her yard he was tense again, but it was shyness.

Her mother was alone in the kitchen. She had just come

in from working in the orchard and was washing her hands at the sink. Helen told her she had brought Dick home for tea.

'Well I'd better make myself presentable,' she said, 'as you're staying.' She was wearing her working jeans. She went over to Helen and held both her cheeks in her hands in a sort of theatrical affection and said, 'The best cups and saucers, daughter.'

'Mother!' said Helen, warningly.

As she left the room she slapped Helen's backside. 'Come on then, girl, bustle about.'

It was Mrs Johnson who set the pace, as usual.

'In the kitchen!' she said when she came down and saw the kitchen table laid for tea.

'Well you'd have only made fun of me if I'd set the table in the other room,' said Helen.

'I bet you don't get treated like that in Dick's house. Does she?' she said to Dick.

'Nothing wrong with the kitchen,' he said.

'Especially for a little cuddle when there's nobody at home.'

'If you don't stop it, Mother!' said Helen.

'Well, my girl, what will you do?' Mrs Johnson was enjoying herself.

'I'll tell Dad.'

'Fat lot of good that'll do you.'

And when he came in Mr Johnson was much the most silent of them all. After he had said a few words he began to read a newspaper.

'Father, take that paper off the table!' said his wife.

'Sorry,' he said, 'force of habit.'

'You're full of them,' said Mrs Johnson.

'What?'

'Bad habits.'

He laughed. 'I don't know why I married her,' he said
to Dick. It was acceptance. Dick relaxed. A calmness
seeped into him, flooding in to obliterate all his anxieties.

And afterwards, in the late evening, he and Helen wan-
dered up the drove between the orchards. He felt differ-
ently about this place now. It was as though he was coming to it new. The squat trees in their straight rows had no
mystery. This was a working place, an apple factory.

He was thinking this as they stepped beyond the orchards and it was only out of the corner of his eye that he
saw Helen shudder. He turned his head.

'It's nothing,' she said. If he no longer felt the trail,
then they were free of it. She had shuddered because she
was expecting it.

But he understood. He stopped and turned back, sensing his way. When he was sure he had passed the place he
turned and looked at her. He raised his arms and let them
fall. 'Nothing,' he said. 'It's gone.'

The sun was going down, slanting their shadows along
the grass. She came towards him, all fear gone, smiling.

The trail caught her in full view of him. Nothing could
disguise it.

'Stop!'

She obeyed, standing within the chill, feeling the misery of it. He came quickly alongside her. There was surprise in his face. 'Nothing,' he said. 'I can't feel it any
more!'

And suddenly she knew why. Slowly she brought a
leaden arm up to the breast pocket of his shirt. Inside it
was the little bottle. She took it out and, like a current of

electricity, warmth tingled along her arm and into her whole body. But she had made him defenceless. The head that had stooped to see what she did stayed down and his limbs were rigid.

She pulled him clear. They had not yet finished with the log. There was power in it, and danger. They had one tiny weapon against it.

But still Helen fought against belief. 'It's only because Mrs Knowles has made us believe it,' she said. 'If she hadn't told us . . .'

'But she did, and she believes it,' he said. 'It'll kill her if we don't stop it.'

'But it's getting dark,' she said, and she was ashamed at her cowardice.

'Then the quicker the better.'

She ran with him to the house.

'Where are you off to now?' Her mother's voice through the open door.

'We won't be late.' Helen hoped her voice did not sound like a wail.

'I'll bring her back,' said Dick.

'See you do.'

Mrs Johnson's voice reached them as they went through the gate. It was like a welcome light on a dark night and they were leaving it behind.

29

They raced the sun but they had started too late. Its fat face was low and red, already sliding down behind the horizon directly ahead of them, far too far ever to catch. It winked and was gone, leaving a blush like a grin in the sky to mock them as they scratched their path like insects over the intolerable vastness of the fen.

'I can't keep up!' Helen was gasping.

Dick slowed, panting. 'You're right,' he said. 'Why panic?' As they rode his mind had become ice cold. They were trapped in another person's fantasies. Mrs Knowles had told them about the body; Mrs Knowles had invented the Silver Fields; the dark and the light were in her mind.

'You've got the bottle?' he said.

'Yes.'

An aspirin bottle filled with water. What was he thinking of? This was madness. A lump of wood that was evil? Madness. A trail? Self-delusion. He was mad. He felt sick.

'It's that man,' he said. 'That damned Miller! He started all this! He's using her!' He hated him. He loathed Mrs Knowles for being a gullible, hysterical lunatic.

'Let's go back.' Helen knew he was heading for a confrontation to ease the shame of being overawed by Miller.

'No! I can do him this time, and then I'm finished with both of them. Finish, finish, finish!'

A battle, a victory. And then an end. He rode into town, taking his time now, preparing words.

'I don't understand you,' said Helen. 'I don't know what you intend to do!'

'You'll find out. Just watch and listen.'

They turned into the Avenues where the street lights hung white in the high green leaves.

'Pretty, isn't it?' he said.

His contempt was cold.

They left their bikes in the hedge again. It seemed the proper thing to do. A small, sane act.

'Come on.' He had a harsh voice when he chose. He plunged into the dark driveway. Helen stumbled after him. Miller's car was where she had last seen it, but glinting now in the light coming from the window over the door. It was malevolent.

Dick banged at the door. An exclamation inside, then feet running downstairs. The door was hurled back and Miller towered there with the hall light above him deepening the dark vertical lines of his face.

'I want to see Mrs Knowles.' Dick faced him squarely.

'You infuriating scoundrel!' Miller blazed fury. 'Get away from here! Out!'

The door was about to slam. Dick lunged. Wood and shoulder thudded. 'I am going to see her!'

'Out!'

The man grabbed his shirt. Face to face. Force against force.

'I am going to see her before you kill her!' Dick's hand came up and grabbed the man's wrist. He wrenched and thrust and Miller was forced half a step back into the yellow light of the hall.

And then Helen saw Miller's face clearly for the first time. Not fury. Horror and shock. And in a flash, the truth.

'Dick!' she shouted. She stepped forward and snatched at his shirt, but the power that possessed him pulled her with him. 'You're wrong!'

All three within the lip of the hall. Only Miller's grasp on the door held them.

'You're wrong!' she yelled again.

Dick's hand held the hard wrist at his neck. Still locked face to face. 'He has the log!'

'No!' she cried. 'No! She brought it here! Mrs Knowles!'

The group swayed. The centre of it, Dick, shook as his own energy turned against him, surging inwards to attack his core.

Miller pushed him, pushed gently, forcing him back.

'Now go away!' Still venom in Miller's voice but he spoke quietly.

'The log.' Dick's voice was feeble, a flag sinking.

'She removed it because she thought it was threatening me. But it turned against her. That is what she believed. Tomorrow I destroy it. Now you know everything.'

Dick released his grip. His hand fell away. Helen, drawing him with her, said, 'Where is Mrs Knowles?'

'She is upstairs, asleep. Under sedation. Now kindly go away. This nonsense must cease.'

They backed away. Miller stood at the door with the light behind him. He held his shoulders squarely, but as though with an effort. He was still watching when they lost sight of him. They were outside in the Avenues when they heard the door close.

They leant in the hedge. Helen was gasping and shuddering. She heard Dick laughing quietly to himself, at himself.

'So now you see,' she said.

'Yes I see. I've been made a fool of.'

'No,' she said. 'You can't blame yourself. You can't blame anybody. Nobody is to blame.'

'What made her do it?' he asked.

'Her husband's not been dead long.' Helen spoke softly. 'And she's been living in that big house all alone.'

'Yes.' Dick heaved himself out of the hedge. 'Ah well she's got Miller now, so all will be well I suppose.'

'I suppose so.'

'Well it's been a long and funny story. It'll make old Jim laugh. At me.'

'There you go again,' said Helen. 'Blaming yourself.'

'Come on,' said Dick. 'Let's go and find somebody.'

But there was nobody at the park gate. An anti-climax.

'Still got the bottle?' he asked.

'Yes.'

'Going to keep it?' He was laughing, still bitter.

'Yes.'

'Don't tell Jim about that.'

She had no intention of telling anybody.

They began to walk across the park towards the single lamp that stood in the centre of the big field. It was dim, tarnished.

'But there are some things I'll never understand,' Dick said. 'There *was* a trail, you know, and it wasn't just water-divining.' He was reluctant to let go of the mystery.

'There are some things that none of us will ever understand,' she said.

'Now that's a profound remark.' He looked at her. She was offended. 'Sorry,' he said. 'Joke.' He put his arm out towards her. She brushed it away.

They reached the far side of the park and began cycling slowly away.

'Helen.'

'What?'

'One more thing. I want to see that log once more before he burns it.'

'Go and ask him tomorrow. He's not bad really.'

'No. Now.'

She did not think he was serious. 'Well you go alone.'

'O.K.' He drew up at the kerb and dismounted. 'Wait for me. I won't be a minute.'

'Where are you going?' She was alarmed and puzzled. They were nowhere near the Avenues.

'See that?' He pointed to a passageway between two fences. 'It leads to Miller's back gate.'

'Don't go.'

'There's nothing to be frightened of. We know the log doesn't mean anything now, except to Mrs Knowles. I just want to make sure I'm free of it.' He took the lamp from his bicycle.

'I'm going home.'

He did not give her threat a chance. 'Hang on just a minute,' he called and he turned quickly and vanished into the dark mouth of the passage.

She stood in the road. The fool. This time he would go alone. Always a dare with him; everything a dare, like that first time with the boat. He nearly killed himself then.

'Oh!' She heard herself gasp. She bit her lip. It was no use; she had to be with him.

In the dark passage she felt her way along the rough boards. A corner. She edged round it and listened. The night was dead silent.

'Dick!' Her whisper was feeble. 'Dick!' No response. She crept further, feeling along the planks with her hands.

Then, on her left, a gap. A gate hung open and, through leaves, she saw a glimmer of light. She turned into the path inside. This was the one. She tried to whisper his name again but the thump of her heart closed her throat.

The conservatory. She saw it dimly. And beyond it the french windows showed light through open curtains. Closer. She licked her lips.

'Dick!' So soft it was barely audible. But as she said it she saw him. His shadow first, stretching out along the grass where the light from the windows lay in long squares. Then his head silhouetted as he craned forward to look inside.

She was ready for the yell of fury as Miller saw him. She was ready to scream herself. But Dick's head, slow as a tortoise, drew back into the shadows and she heard him creeping away.

'Dick!'

The faint sound of moving stopped.

'Helen!' His whisper answered, and he came up to her quickly. Too much noise. Then he bent his head towards hers. 'Miller's asleep,' he said. 'Flat out.' He had seen him in an armchair, sprawled out, head lolling.

Dick seemed to be enjoying himself. 'The trail's still here,' he said, 'up the path where she brought the thing. I can still feel it or smell it or something.'

He led her to the glass door. 'Good,' he said over his shoulder, 'still open.'

'Be careful!' she pleaded.

'I'm glad you came,' he said. 'I still feel this thing pretty strongly. Got your magic water in case I faint?'

He was confident. One diminishing fear to beat and he was free. He pushed the door open softly. Sea smell, mud smell. He shivered but he could conquer it. There was enough light to see the white furniture. Helen strained her eyes, seeking among the shadows on the floor. She jumped when the lamp in Dick's hand sent its beam prodding, shielded by his hand, down to their feet. He moved it over the uneven bricks of the floor. She clung to his arm.

The Turkey carpet was where they had left it. But it lay flat. Their beam darted over its endless red and blue zig-zag. The log had gone.

While Miller slept.

The horror crawled over them as they ran; crawled like Mrs Knowles creeping down while Miller slept. Out along this path she had walked hugging the log while Miller slept.

No need for trail-following. No need for them to take her roundabout route along the little roads. Through the thin night traffic they sped for the bridge.

'Wait!' Dick's call made them slither to a stop. He stepped on to the pavement. The river dimpled its ugly face under the moon. He was shivering before he felt the chill of the trail.

'She's been across!' One danger less; not death by drowning.

Along the brink where the huge curve was moon-shadowed, colonnade of an empty city. Nothing stirred. The cold air bit their cheeks as they leant into it.

The black iron gate was ajar. They ran over the gravel, jumped the steps and lunged at the door. Without a fraction of movement from itself it threw them back piti-lessly. They thrust at the bell and banged on the faceless panels. The door of a tomb. And where the log had rested on the step they stood as cold as death.

'Round the back!'

The moon was on them. Lit by ghost-light they forced the latch of the gate and went through. Slower now, sensing that stealth was necessary where banging and alarms had failed, they crept through the long garden. The lightest of breezes stirred the tops of the trees and made them surge like a sea in the sky.

The house rose before them. Useless to try doors. Dick wrapped his handkerchief round his fist and selected a panel of glass. A small crash, a clatter of falling glass, and his hand was reaching for the key inside. He turned it and withdrew his arm. The door opened towards them. He went in with Helen following.

No torch. He had forgotten it.

'Her husband's room!' The words carried to him on the top of her breath.

Was she here? No. The moon struck down on the floor by their feet. Everything was still.

They crossed to the black alcove and Dick felt for the door handle. The heavy door swung inwards without a sound. Their owl-eyes saw the chequered floor of the hall, but dimly. The next clue lay on the strict squares of the tiles.

Dick reached for Helen's hand. Warm in spite of her fear. As soft as a puppy.

Together they moved out from under the curve of the stairs, into the open but caged by the circular walls and the spiralling stairs that curved around a column of unreachable space above them.

They shuffled forward, casting about for the invisible

path. They found it at the foot of the stairs. Like a slug's trail.

They climbed. The carpet was thick. They trod softly. Past the first window where the surge of the trees sent dappled moonlight over their feet like foam.

Upwards, curving to the dark side. A black window with nothing outside but a straight drop, the road and the river.

One more flight to the balcony.

They paused.

They were made to pause; held back.

A rustle. A faint rustle was caught under the shell of the dome and went whispering above them. Round and round until it died.

'Mrs Knowles!' Dick's voice in the hollow of the great dark trumpet. The shadows ate it.

'Quick!'

Up the slug's trail together. Up into the darkness under the balcony. And through it into the giddy light of the high window at the back of the house.

And one window opposite. Dark except for the stars. Darker than it should have been because of a shape against it.

'Mrs Knowles!' Across the space.

A scrambling sound. The shape changed, seemed to dip. They ran round the balcony, leaning, leaning over the drop.

And below, at the bottom of the well, a hammering and a voice shouting, shut out, muffled.

They hurled themselves at her, caught her as she leant out, tipping into space. Back against the wall they held her, one each side. She struggled, hard fingers, hard arms in the darkness.

179

'Tell her!' Helen's voice over the diving, writhing head.

'Into the moonlight!' he said.

They forced her to walk between them to the bright window. They looked out over the tossing waves of tree-tops. Out into the distance for her Silver Fields. Nothing under the moon but the dark distance. Helen lifted her hand in front of them. She twisted the little bottle in the moonlight, making it glint as she spoke.

'We found the Silver Fields! We found them this morning! We took this water from them!'

Suddenly, behind and above them, lights sprang on, dimming the moonlight. They looked over their shoulders, startled.

Directly opposite, across the space, the log stood. Facing them. Quite still. Utterly sinister.

Mrs Knowles twisted, whimpering. Dick forced both her arms behind her back, gave her to Helen and snatched the bottle.

'Hold her!'

He ran. It was like flying, circling under the dome, swooping on his prey. He snatched at the black-green hair. snarling, hate mounting over fear.

'Mrs Knowles!' A yell to pull her eyes across the space. 'Mrs Knowles! I kill this thing with the power of the Silver Fields!' He raised his right hand high and in his fist the glass gleamed. Struck down. Smashed with a sword stroke at the smooth helmet head. In his hand the glass shattered. Water and blood.

And failure. The log stood.

And disgust. The clammy hair he held began to tear away from the dead head. Tore away as slowly the log leant away from him, leant over the balcony railing, tilted away, upended and slid into space.

They watched it go. They watched it turn slowly like a sailor buried at sea, going down alone.

And Mrs Knowles screamed. Free of Helen, leaning over the rail, screaming down beyond the black log to a small grey figure moving out on to the black and white tiles to meet his fate.

Miller looked up.

Everything sharp. He saw her face far away under the dome, terrified in a helpless dream, warning him, warning him. And between, a bird of death, black wings wide, plunging to kill.

It needed but one step. He held her eyes. He despised the bird. He stepped slowly back. The wing of the bird swept past his face. At his feet the log burst itself into black fragments and stank.

She was running downstairs. Spiralling down to him.

High above, on the ring of the balcony, two small figures stood at the edge of the dome. They saw the grey man hold the woman and heard a faint murmur, wordless as water, drift up from the bottom of the well.

The green weed was in his hand. He brushed it off. He circled to stand beside her in front of the bright window. They looked out. The fen was flat, but never anywhere as flat as the sea. It absorbed the moon and hoarded it in shadows, except just below them where the tree-tops, reaching for the sky, frothed to make the undersides of their leaves shine silver like waves coming in to lie down on a beach.

30

They came down slowly. A slow spiral down to earth. Mrs Knowles and Miller had gone off into a side room and they were alone.

The log lay in black fragments. They went closer. The rounded end had rolled clear. Dick stood over it, all fear gone.

Helen looked down at the shattered pieces. She knew what it was before he did. She saw the clenched fist and the splintered sword; the broken, spreadeagled bones of the ancient body.

She pointed, and the movement of her hand drew his eyes. He saw the finger bones welded to the rusted iron. A clump of fist; jagged metal – death dealers. The danger had been real. He shrank within himself, and then he felt Helen's hand in his. The danger was dead.

He looked at the severed head. One last dare. He put his foot out to roll it over.

'Leave it!' Miller stood at the door behind them. 'Leave it.' Not a command, a request. 'I shall remove it.' He came towards them. There was a difference in him, a gentleness they had not seen. 'She wants to see you,' he said.

But none of them moved. They stood looking down at the broken bones.

'It was a body,' said Dick.

'I know,' Miller sighed. 'But she doesn't know,' he said. 'May I ask you not to tell her?'

'We won't,' said Dick.

'She'll never ever know,' said Helen.

Miller sighed again and stooped to pick up the sword by what was left of the blade. He tapped the hilt on the floor and the finger bones fell away. He stood up. 'This I shall keep,' he said. They knew why. It helped to prove his theory.

'King John's Treasure is down there in the mud,' said Dick.

'Possibly.' Miller was almost smiling.

'Aren't you going to tell anybody?' Dick knew that a theory proved meant more to him than jewels.

'I may do,' said Miller. 'One day.' He looked down, frowning. 'But now I'm going to do a criminal act.' He stirred a black fragment with his foot. 'This has got to be removed, lost for good. Her sanity depends on it.'

'There was magic in it,' said Dick. Miller's eyes glanced at him, glinting. Dick willed Miller to keep his eyes on him and won. 'There was magic in it,' he said again. 'How else do you account for the trail?'

'I do not account for the trail,' said Miller. 'All I know is that you seemed to know what was in her mind.'

It was painful for him to say that. It was he himself who should have read her mind. Helen wanted to bring him some comfort. 'Does she know she brought the log here herself?' It was still the log to her; it always would be.

'I think so,' said Miller. 'She thought she was protecting me from it. It represented a curse from the past. But her own mind turned it against herself.'

He inclined his head towards the door. He wanted them to go in to her.

She sat by the empty fireplace under the overhang of

the marble cliff. She was small. She and Miller were both small, emptied. Her eyes were closed but she knew they were there. They crossed the room and stood looking down on her. She was waiting, letting her senses feel out beyond them, waiting for something.

At their backs there was space. They felt the emptiness of it and heard movements in the hall where Miller was gathering up the rottenness of the dead nightmare. The front door opened and closed. The sounds ceased. There was a long pause.

Her eyelids trembled.

'It's gone!' she said softly.

Her eyes opened. They were blue but very dark. Deep in them a pain was still struggling, but very deep now, ebbing.

Suddenly she clenched her fists. The pain came back in a wave. She gazed up at them, startled.

All the force of her fear yawned open and Dick, caught on the edge, began to slip down in to it; the river of fear rippling its lips over his skin.

Helen saw him going from her, drowning in the panic of Mrs Knowles. Her anger came from within, bursting out white and brighter than the moon.

'Dick!' She clawed at the shoulder of his shirt and spun him round. The cloth tore. His face was as pale as the skin of his shoulder. Her mind reached for him, reached out, touched and held. She drew him back, slowly guiding him, ignoring and despising the woman until the panic spilled from his face and he saw her.

Mrs Knowles was standing beside them. She was calm. 'Take him away now,' she said.

Miller stood at the door.

'I've thrown that thing in the river,' he said. 'It's gone.'

'The river,' said Mrs Knowles.

'The tide is going out,' said Miller. 'You'll never see it again.'

'No,' she said. 'Never again.' She stood beside them and her head bowed and she began to weep, quite quietly, with her hands by her side.

Miller came up to her, a tall, grey, gentle man. He put his arm around her shoulder.

They looked at him.

'It's over,' he said to them. 'You ended it for her.'

It was necessary to leave. They would meet again, at some calm time.

They went out of the room and closed the door. The hall was quiet and cold. They crossed to where the log had struck. The cold, hard tiles had flung it off without a mark.

Dick looked for a broken lock on the front door. There was no sign it had been forced. Miller had used a key. The big door swung to behind them. Within the heavy wood the lock clicked home.

He rode home with her, out across the fens as the moon sank out of sight. They said little. It was as though they were still moving in the corridors of a stranger's mind.

Her house was in darkness. They left their bicycles at her gate and walked along the drove. The orchard trees were dark and secret. He saw the glimmer of her face in the darkness.

'Will the trail still be there?' he said.

She said nothing until they were at the orchard edge and then she made him stop. She went out alone, her white dress fading into the darkness until she was as vague as a moth.

Her voice came to him through the quiet night. 'Come out and see.'

He went towards her. She was a fragile, wavering shape, unreachable.

He moved nearer. Dimly he saw the shadows of her mouth and of her eyes. Closer. He felt her breath.

A faint rustle in the grass of the night. His skin was on the point of shivering. It may have been the trail.

Also in the Plus series

IF IT WEREN'T FOR SEBASTIAN
Jean Ure

Maggie's decision to break the family tradition of studying science at university in favour of a course in shorthand-typing causes a major row. But the rift with her parents is nothing to the difficulties she meets when unpredictable Sebastian enters her life.

A PARCEL OF PATTERNS
Jill Paton Walsh

It is Mall who tells of the tragedy of the fearful plague coming to her village, possibly brought from London by a parcel of dress patterns. She tells dramatically and powerfully of how the villagers lived and died, and their collective heroism in containing the disease. But this is also a moving love-story, for Mall must not go to meet her beloved Thomas, for fear of passing the sickness on to him.

MARTINI-ON-THE-ROCKS
Susan Gregory

Eight very funny, chaotic, true-to-life stories about a bunch of typical teenagers. They fall in love, get into trouble, chat, tease, laugh and have great fun. Anybody who's ever been to school cannot fail to be entertained!

EASY CONNECTIONS
Liz Berry

Some people say Cathy is a brilliant painter with an exceptional future ahead of her. But from the day when she unwittingly trespasses on the country estate of rock star Paul Devlin, she becomes a changed character. Beautiful, cold and violent, Dev is captivated by Cathy, while she is attracted and repelled in equal measure. However, Dev usually gets what he wants . . . An unusual love story set in the vivid worlds of rock music and art.

LET THE CIRCLE BE UNBROKEN
Mildred D. Taylor

For Cassie Logan, 1935 in the American deep south is a time of bewildering change: the Depression is tightening its grip, rich and poor are in conflict and racial tension is increasing. As she grows away from the security of childhood, Cassie struggles to understand the turmoil around her and the reasons for the deep-rooted fears of her family and friends.

THE VILLAGE BY THE SEA
Anita Desai

Hari and his sister Lila are the eldest children of an Indian family. Their mother is ill and their father spends most of his time in a drunken stupor. Grimly, Lila and Hari struggle to hold the family together until one day, in a last-ditch attempt to break out of the poverty, Hari leaves his sisters in the silent shadowy hut and runs off to Bombay. This is the story of how Hari and Lila cope with the harsh realities of life in city and village.

FUTURETRACK 5
Robert Westall

Henry Kitson lives in the twenty-first century, where success is determined by being good – not too good – and by a willingness to conform. Those who don't make it are consigned through the Wire, lobotomized or, in Kitson's case, allocated to Tech – a small body of people who maintain the computers. It's not much of a life. But meeting bike champion Keri is a turning point for Kitson and the two form an uneasy friendship to find out just what makes the system tick.

THE HAUNTING OF CHAS McGILL AND OTHER STORIES
Robert Westall

Eight supernatural tales to send shivers down your spine! Some are weird and mysterious, where Chas McGill comes face to face with a soldier from the past. Others are more sinister, and some are disturbingly *possible* – all very different but with one thing in common: the ability to make your skin crawl!

NOAH'S CASTLE
John Rowe Townsend

In lawless and hungry Britain, delivery trucks need a police escort. With the price of a tin of sardines at £200, soldiers patrol the streets of the cities, ready to fire at looters and raiding parties. Norman Mortimer has decided to protect his family by converting his home into a larder. But can they hold out against the violent gangs, and survive the pressures building up within?